Ernest Abraham Hart

Hypnotism, Mesmerism and the New Witchcraft

Ernest Abraham Hart

Hypnotism, Mesmerism and the New Witchcraft

ISBN/EAN: 9783337369873

Printed in Europe, USA, Canada, Australia, Japan

Cover: Foto ©Andreas Hilbeck / pixelio.de

More available books at **www.hansebooks.com**

HYPNOTISM, MESMERISM

AND THE

NEW WITCHCRAFT

BY

ERNEST HART

FORMERLY SURGEON TO THE WEST LONDON HOSPITAL
AND OPHTHALMIC SURGEON TO ST MARY'S HOSPITAL LONDON

A NEW EDITION, ENLARGED

WITH CHAPTERS ON 'THE ETERNAL GULLIBLE'
AND NOTE ON THE HYPNOTISM OF 'TRILBY'

WITH 24 ILLUSTRATIONS

LONDON
SMITH, ELDER, & CO., 15 WATERLOO PLACE
1896

PREFACE

THE SECOND EDITION

———◦◦———

THIS little book has for some time been out of print, and as a considerable portion of its contents necessarily is of only more or less ephemeral interest, I had not intended to republish it. I have, however, received so many letters of inquiry from correspondents, both here and on the other side of the Atlantic, as to the probable date of a new edition, that it is clear there is still a considerable demand for the book. I hope I am not wrong in interpreting this as a sign that the public at large is becoming more and more penetrated with the conviction that Hypnotism, when it is not a pernicious fraud, is a mere futility which should have no place in the life of those who have work to do in the world.

In the present edition a chapter has been added embodying the confessions of a professional medium. Some new matter has also been placed in the Appendix. Otherwise the little book is unchanged.

January 1896.

PREFACE

THE FIRST EDITION

———◦✧◦———

THE papers here brought together have recently appeared in the 'Nineteenth Century' and the 'British Medical Journal,' and are reprinted by permission. They are published to meet the wishes of some who have suggested to me that it might prove useful and acceptable that they should be collected into a small volume, and thus become more available for current reference than they would otherwise have been. They were so favourably received at the time of publication, that I may venture to hope it is not presumptuous to give them this more permanent shape. Nothing has been written in the way of criticism which seemed to me at all substantial, or to call for

a

any modification of the text; so that while I can hardly hope that their somewhat aggressive tone will pass altogether without disapproval from a certain school of psychical researchers, yet I may venture to think that they will now, as they did when first published, meet with general acceptance from the medical and scientific world, and that they will serve a useful purpose in dissipating some popular errors and a good deal of pseudo-scientific superstition, superimposed on a slender basis of physiological and pathological phenomena. They may be of some service, also, in unmasking a prevalent system of imposture which had imposed upon a good many journalists and men of literary culture.

ERNEST HART.

38 WIMPOLE STREET, W.
March 1893.

CONTENTS

HYPNOTISM AND HUMBUG [1]

The Attraction of the Unknown—The Early History of Mesmerism—
Some Control-experiments—Natural Sleep and Hypnotic Sleep—
Hypnotism of Animals—The Follies of Telepathy and of
'Animal Magnetism.'

THE unknown has always had a great attraction for
every class of mind, and whoever promises to lift for
us the veil of the mysterious and to afford us a glimpse
into the unknown world may always count upon a large
following. It is the infirmity of great minds as of
small. The poet, the mystic, the imaginative philo-
sopher, share its higher privileges; the charlatan, the
quack, and the stage performer, its greater profits
There is one phase of the pursuit of the unknown, and
one method of manipulating it, which has had the privilege of exciting the interest and inflaming the imagination of mankind in all periods of history, in every phase
of civilisation, and in every part of the world; probably
even amongst prehistoric peoples, and certainly amongst
aboriginal savages. It is the endeavour to search out
hidden forces and mysterious qualities of the mind—to
discover other methods of transmitting mental impres-

---

[1] An Address delivered in Toynbee Hall.

sions than those of sight, speech, and touch; other
avenues than those of the five senses; and other means
of mental influence than those everywhere known and
visible. It is with this quest, and with some of its
ancient vestiges and strange modern developments,
that I purpose to deal. Hypnotism, which is now
the subject of much intelligent and well-directed
modern research, and is also, unfortunately, the play-
thing of a class of wandering stage performers, is the
lineal descendant of many ancient beliefs. It was
known to the earliest races of Asia and amongst the
Persian Magi; and to this day the Yogis and Fakirs of
India throw themselves into a state of hypnotic ecstasy
and reverie by fixation of gaze. In many convents
of the Greek Church it has been practised since the
eleventh century, as it is still by the Omphalopsychics,
by whom hypnotic reverie is obtained by steadily
gazing at the umbilicus. Modern hypnotism, mesmerism, telepathy, animal magnetism, thought-reading, and
thought-transference are of the family which in earlier
times, and when men were less wont to analyse natural
phenomena by rational methods, brought forth the practices of the Magians, the antics of the demoniacs and
the possessed, the expulsion of evil spirits by exorcism,
the healing of the king's-evil by laying on of hands, the
serious acceptance and judicial punishment of the hallucinations of the witches, and the fantastic cruelty of
the witch-finders. The proceedings by which Sarchas,
the faithful companion of Apollonius, gave sight to the

blind, movement to the paralysed, hearing to the deaf, and reason to the insane, were essentially methods of what we should now call ' suggestion '; and the application of the influence of suggestion to persons in the most various mental and physical states, whether of health or disease, will serve to throw light on some of the most tragic, blood-stained, picturesque, and incredible pages of history, as well as on a multitude of stage tricks and quack procedures which are now, as they have been at frequent intervals during the last century, much in vogue. But first of all I must summarise some of the related facts in the physiology of the brain, and give a little of my own personal experience as an investigator, an experience which led me to take special interest in the subject.

Very early in life I was brought into contact with a well-known physician, the late Dr. Elliotson, who, unfortunately for himself, was victimised by two characteristic specimens of that kind of hysterical impostors who delight in deceiving investigators of mesmerism, hypnotism, spiritualism, and the like, and whose great object is to become either centres of interest and notoriety or to make money. Although a very able and earnest man, Dr. Elliotson was completely entrapped and deceived by two women named Okey, who were his patients in University College Hospital. They made him believe that when he had thrown them into what was called the mesmeric sleep, they could read letters in a sealed envelope placed on the surface of their bodies, their eyes being previously carefully bandaged. Although the trick was thoroughly exposed by the late Mr. Wakley, coroner for Middlesex, and Dr. Elliotson had to retire from University College Hospital, he had seen enough of the actual and indubitable phenomena of induced sleep which he was able to produce, to lead him to devote the rest of his life to the endeavour to employ this means of inducing sleep, as a curative agent. He attended a very near and dear relative of mine who was suffering from a chronic and painful affection of the joints, which murdered rest. He was successful in giving her sleep at nights; and this striking demonstration of an actual power, which, if not resident in, was at least connected with his method of practice, not only made me grateful to him, but sufficed to impel me, when later I entered into the medical profession, to test his methods. I very soon found that in a large number of cases there is no difficulty whatever in producing what we may call, though not very accurately, artificial sleep. I found that I could produce it easily and frequently by means of what were then called mesmeric passes, with the hands or by desiring the patient to look fixedly at my eyes; and, at first, following the directions of Elliotson and of his master Mesmer, I at the same time exercised my will, and 'willed' the patients whom I mesmerised, to sleep. Just at this time there were springing up two other methods of exciting this artificial condition, one being widely known as Braidism, because it was practised by Dr. Braid, and the other as electro-biology—a name which had, I believe, been first given to it in America, about 1848, by a New Englander named Grimes. The latter method had been lectured on, under the title of Electrical Psychology, in 1850, by Dr. Dodds, before the Congress of the United States, in reply to a semi-official invitation from some members of the Senate. These lectures had been published, under the title of the ' Philosophy of Electrical Psychology,' in New York, and been disseminated in England in 1850, when I first took to studying the subject, by Dr. Darling and others, amongst whom Dr. B. W. Carpenter, Sir James Simpson, Sir Henry Holland, and Sir David Brewster were perhaps the best-known personages.

At this stage of my career I was house surgeon to a metropolitan hospital, and I had rather a sharp reminder of the danger of meddling with a subject of this nature. Two friends—one of whom, I may say parenthetically, was a member of the last Government—were spending the evening in my rooms at the hospital, and with them was a lady who professed the customary incredulity as to my powers of inducing sleep. She submitted herself as subject, and was very soon mesmerised ; and so prolonged and complete was her slumber, that she was with difficulty aroused ; and when she left, her gait was tottering and she had to be supported on either side by her friends. This occurrence was reported to the hospital authorities by an unfriendly official, with very hostile suggestions. I was summoned before the board, I gave my explanation, and the matter was referred to the Medical Committee. I escaped with a solemn and incredulous admonition—chiefly, I think, because I was rather a favourite pupil, with a good record in the school—the sort of verdict being ' not guilty, but don't do it again,' pronounced with a dubious smile and a severe shake of the head, which clearly conveyed that my censors were very far from accepting the scientific explanation of the facts. I could recount a long series of what might sound like strange stories of my various experiences. They were enough to show that the condition induced partook of the character, sometimes of ordinary sleep, sometimes of cataleptic trance, sometimes of waking somnambulism. The persons acted on were very much under the influence of suggestion, and could be made to say and do all sorts of strange and ridiculous things—to reply to questions in which they revealed various secrets, to obey commands which at any other time and under any other circumstances they would be very unwilling to fulfil, to perform acts which were senseless, and even dangerous, unless I had exercised special precautions ; as to jump from heights, to dive off a table on to the floor as if swimming, to attack with a dagger an imaginary enemy, to flee from supposititious serpents or stinging insects in an agony of fear, to listen to imaginary nightingales in an ecstasy of pleasure, and all these performances took place without consciousness at the time or memory afterwards.

The subjects were reduced, in fact, to the condition of human automata, capable of being acted upon by an external will which they were unable to resist. But at a very early stage I asked myself what was the real meaning of all this, and how far it was possible to analyse the origin and to define the sphere of these phenomena; and I instituted for myself a series of control-experiments.

I will briefly explain what is meant by control-experiments; for if all who investigate or make any sort of research into what are called psychical phenomena would carefully consider what are the kinds of control-experiments necessary to verify the true causation of the results of their research, the lamentable confusion, the tissue of errors, and the foggy mysticism with which this subject is still surrounded would be in large part dispelled. The attractiveness of the pursuit for many minds would, no doubt, also be proportionately diminished; and it may, indeed, be doubted whether, under a system of rigid control-tests, such a society as the Society for Psychical Research would find material sufficiently diverting to the many to enable it to continue long to exist. The control-experiments which I instituted consisted in eliminating precisely those elements which were supposed to be the efficient causes of the phenomena produced. Thus, the first and most efficient of the causes of this mesmeric, hypnotic, magnetic, or electro-biological condition of the subject was generally assumed to be either the will-power of the operator or some fluid, magnetic, electrical, psychical, or other, emanating from the operator, or from some object which he had touched, or otherwise impregnated or invested with an influence, a fluid, or a power proceeding from himself. The mesmeric state was supposed by Mesmer himself to be due to something which he called a magnetic fluid. At the time when all Paris rang with the wonders of his power, and when his antechambers were filled with princes of the blood royal, with the halt, the lame and the blind, with mystics, monks, and *religieuses*, with ladies of fashion and the heterogeneous multitude who love the marvellous ; he had constructed huge and complex tubs filled with bottles of fluid erroneously called electrical fluid, such as Count Mattei now dispenses, and connected by a complicated system of wires with handles, to be held by his subjects. Mesmer received 16,000*l.* for telling his secrets, which, of course, turned out to be no secrets at all, and it was found there was no electricity in the bottles or the tubs. Presently he retired across the Rhine enriched by his dupes, who ceased to be cured as the fashion died away and as their faith waned. In all these so-called magnetic cures, faith-cures, and Mattei specifics, Perkins tractors and electric belts, you must make haste to be cured while the faith or the fashion lasts ; as it fades, they cease to cure. But Mesmer left a doctrine, a principle, and a nomenclature which has served the purpose of succeeding generations of quacks and *gobemouches*. The first thing I did, then, was to ascertain whether there was anything electrical or magnetic in the phenomena. This was very soon answered in the negative. The most delicate electrical instruments failed to detect any difference whatever either in my own electrical state or in that of the persons operated on, at any stage of the proceedings. The ordinary methods of conducting or of cutting off magnetic or electric currents neither favoured nor interfered with the results. The interposition of silk or of glass, the insulation of the subject or of myself, did not in any way modify the phenomena, which were evidently entirely independent of the magnetic or electric fluid. And here I may remark that this has always been found to be the case whenever tests have been applied to the so-called animal magnetisers or electro-biologists and their subjects. The fact is, that the word 'animal magnetism' applied to any of these phenomena of induced sleep, human automatism, hypnotic suggestion, or faith-cure, is a pure misnomer. It is an example of that tendency satirised by Voltaire when he speaks of the tendency of mystics and charlatans to consecrate their ignorance and to impose its conclusions upon others *by giving a name which has no meaning to phenomena which they do not understand.* There is, of course, electrical reaction in the living tissues of the body, and all muscular contractions are associated with simultaneous electric changes; but electric fluid has no special relations to nerve rather than to muscle tissue; it has no relation whatever to mental influence. Animal magnetism, in the sense in which it is commonly applied as related to faith-cures, hypnotic performances, and the like, is a term without meaning ; while the whole tribe of self-styled animal magnetisers may be dismissed as conscious or unconscious impostors.

After this parenthesis I return to a second kind of control-experiment. Apart from the magnetic fluid which was supposed to emanate from the magnetiser, there was then, had lived for many years, and still exists, a theory that the will of the operator had much to do with bringing the subjects into a state of fascination or sleep. I therefore eliminated my will in one set of experiments, and in another I set it in direct opposition to the result to be obtained. Thus I dispensed with all passes or gestures, and simply sat in front of my subjects in a mental attitude of indifference and curiosity. I did not will them to sleep, but I allowed them to look at me, or at a coin, or at a silver spoon suspended six inches in front of the eye, or at the tip of their own nose. The same results were attained. I went further. Mesmer, who had mesmerised as many as eight thousand people in one year in Paris, and his disciple Puysegur, had on various occasions mesmerised, as it was termed, the trunk of a tree, and, in virtue of the influences with which the tree was supposed to be thus impregnated, people joining hands and surrounding it, and gazing at it fixedly, had fallen into the mesmeric sleep, or had received the same kind of benefits in their rheumatic, neuralgic, paralytic, and other nervous affections as from the direct treatment of the sage himself. Staying at the well-known country house in Kent of a distinguished London banker, formerly member for Greenwich, I had been called upon to set to sleep, and to arrest a continuous barking cough from which a young lady who was staying in the house was suffering, and who, consequently, was a torment to herself and her friends. I thought this a good opportunity for a control-experiment and I sat her down in front of a lighted candle which I assured her that I had previously mesmerised. Presently her cough ceased and she fell into a profound sleep, which lasted till twelve o'clock next day. When I returned from shooting, I was informed that she was still asleep and could not be awoke, and I had great difficulty in awaking her. That night there was a large dinner-party, and, unluckily, I sat opposite to her. Presently she again became drowsy, and had to be led from the table, alleging, to my great confusion, that I was again mesmerising her. So susceptible did she become to my supposed mesmeric influence, which I vainly assured her, as was the case, that I was very far from exercising or attempting to exercise, that it was found expedient to take her up to London. I was out riding in the afternoon that she left, and as we passed the railway station, my host, who was riding with me, suggested that, as his friends were just leaving by that train, he would like to alight and take leave of them. I dismounted with him and

went on to the platform, and avoided any leave-taking;
but unfortunately in walking up and down it seems
that I twice passed the window of the young lady's car-
riage.   She was again self-mesmerised, and fell into a
sleep which lasted throughout the journey, and recurred
at intervals for some days afterwards.   Such was the history of a candle supposed to be invested with mesmeric
influence, and therefore acting as though it were.   It is
an instructive and a suggestive incident, which I could
parallel with many others, and I dare say it will easily
be seen in what direction it is leading.   I may add
that when I proceeded to a more active and direct
intervention of the will, opposing sleep, the results
were not affected negatively.   So long as the person
operated on believed that my will was that she should
sleep, sleep followed.   The most energetic willing in
my internal consciousness that there should be no sleep
failed to prevent it, where the usual physical methods
of hypnotisation, stillness, repose, a fixed gaze, or the
verbal expression of an order to sleep, were employed.

Thus, then, we have arrived at the point at which
it will be plain that the condition produced in these
cases, and known under a varied jargon invented
either to conceal ignorance, to express false hypo-
theses, or to mask the design of impressing the
imagination and possibly prey upon the pockets of a
credulous and wonder-loving public—such names as
the mesmeric condition, magnetic sleep, clairvoyance,
electro-biology, animal magnetism, faith-trance, and

many other aliases—such a condition, I say, is always subjective. It is independent of passes or gestures; it has no relation to any fluid emanating from the operator; it has no relation to his will, or to any influence which he exercises upon inanimate objects; distance does not affect it, nor proximity, nor the intervention of any conductors or non-conductors, whether silk or glass or stone, or even a brick wall. We can transmit the order to sleep by telephone or by telegraph. We can practically get the same results while eliminating even the operator, if we can contrive to influence the imagination or to affect the physical condition of the subject by any one of a great number of contrivances.

What does all this mean? I will refer to one or two facts in relation to the structure and function of the brain, and show one or two simple experiments of very ancient parentage and date, which will, I think, help to an explanation. First, let us recall something of what we know of the anatomy and localisation of function in the brain, and of the nature of ordinary sleep. The brain, as you know, is a complicated organ, made up internally of nerve masses, or ganglia, of which the central and underlying masses are connected with the automatic functions and involuntary actions of the body, while the investing surface shows a system of complicated convolutions rich in grey matter, thickly sown with microscopic cells in which the nerve ends terminate. At the base of the brain is a complete circle of arteries, from which spring great numbers of small arterial vessels carrying a profuse blood supply throughout the whole mass, and capable of contraction in small tracts, so that small areas of the brain may, at any given moment, become bloodless, while other parts of the brain may simultaneously become highly congested. Now, if the brain, or any part of it, be deprived of the circulation of blood through it, or be rendered partially bloodless, or if it be excessively congested and overloaded with blood, or if it be sub- jected to local pressure, the part of the brain so acted upon ceases to be capable of exercising its functions. The regularity of the action of the brain and the sanity and completeness of the thought which is one of the functions of its activity depend upon the healthy regularity of the quantity of blood passing through all its parts, and upon the healthy quality of the blood so circulating. If we press upon the carotid arteries which pass up through the neck to form the arterial circle of Willis, at the base of the brain, within the skull—of which I have already spoken, and which supplies the brain with blood—we quickly, as everyone knows, produce insensibility. Thought is abolished, consciousness is lost. And if we continue the pressure, all those automatic actions of the body—such as the beating of the heart, the breathing motions of the lung, which maintain life and are controlled by the lower brain centres of ganglia—are quickly stopped, and death ensues.

We know by observation in cases where portions of the skull have been removed, either in men or in animals, that during natural sleep the upper part of the brain—its convoluted surface, which in health and in the waking state is faintly pink like a blushing cheek, from the colour of the blood circulating through the network of capillary arteries—becomes white and almost bloodless. It is in these upper convolutions of the brain, as we also know, that the will and the directing power are resident; so that in sleep the will is abolished and consciousness fades gradually away as the blood is pressed out by the contraction of the arteries. So, also, the consciousness and the directing will may be abolished by altering the quality of the blood passing through the convolutions of the brain. We may intro-duce a volatile substance, such as chloroform, and its first effect will be to abolish consciousness and induce profound slumber and a blessed insensibility to pain. The like effects will follow more slowly upon the absorption of a drug, such as opium; or we may in-duce hallucinations by introducing into the blood other toxic substances, such as Indian hemp or stramonium. We are not conscious of the mechanism producing the arterial contraction and bloodlessness of those convo-lutions related to natural sleep. But we are not altogether without control over them. We can, we know, help to compose ourselves to sleep, as we say in ordinary language. We retire into a darkened room, we relieve ourselves from the stimulus of the special senses, we free ourselves from the influence of noises, of strong light, of powerful odours, or of tactile impressions. We lie down and endeavour to soothe brain-activity by driving away disturbing thoughts, or, as people sometimes say, 'try to think of nothing.' And, happily, we generally succeed more or less well. Some people possess an even more marked control over this mechanism of sleep. I can generally succeed in putting myself to sleep at any hour of the day, either in the library chair or in the brougham. This is, so to speak, a process of self-hypnotisation, and I have often practised it when going from house to house, when in the midst of a busy practice ; and sometimes I have amused my friends and family by exercising this faculty, which I do not think it very difficult to acquire. Now there is something · here which deserves a little further examination, but which it would take too much time to fully develop at present. Most people know something of what is meant by reflex action. The nerves which pass from the various organs to the brain convey with great rapidity messages to its various parts, which are answered by reflected waves of impulse. If the soles of the feet be tickled, contraction of the toes, or involuntary laughter, will be excited, or perhaps only a shuddering and skin-contraction known as goose-skin. The irritation of the nerve end in the skin has carried a message to the involuntary or the voluntary ganglia of the brain, which has responded by reflecting back again nerve-impulses which have contracted the muscles of the feet or the skin-muscles, or have given rise to associated ideas and explosion of laughter. In the same way, if during sleep heat be applied to the soles of the feet, dreams of walking over hot surfaces—Vesuvius or Fusiyama, or still hotter places—may be produced, or dreams of adventure on frozen surfaces or in Arctic regions may be created by applying ice to the feet of the sleeper.

Here, then, it is seen that we have a mechanism in the body, known to physiologists as the ideo-motor or sensory motor system of nerves, which can produce, without the consciousness of the individual, and automatically, a series of muscular contractions. And remember that the coats of the arteries are muscular and contractile under the influence of external stimuli, acting without the help of the consciousness, or when the consciousness is in abeyance. I will give another example of this, which completes the chain of phenomena in the natural brain and the natural body I wish to bring under notice in explanation of the true as distinguished from the false, or falsely interpreted, phenomena of hypnotism, mesmerism, and electro-biology. I will take the excellent illustration quoted by Dr. B. W. Carpenter in his old-time but valuable book on 'The Physiology of the Brain.' When a hungry man sees food, or when, let us say, a hungry boy looks into a cookshop, he becomes aware of a watering of the mouth and a gnawing sensation at the stomach. What does this mean? It

means that the mental impression made upon him by
the welcome and appetising spectacle has caused a
secretion of saliva and of gastric juice ; that is to say,
the brain has, through the ideo-motor set of nerves,
sent a message which has dilated the vessels around
the salivary and gastric glands, increased the flow of
blood through them, and quickened their secretion.
Here we have, then, a purely subjective mental activity
acting through a mechanism of which the boy is quite
ignorant, and which he is unable to control, and producing that action on the vessels of dilatation or contraction which, as we have seen, is the essential
condition of brain activity and the evolution of thought,
and is related to the quickening or the abolition of
consciousness, and to the activity or abeyance of
function in the will-centres and upper convolutions of
the brain, as in its other centres of localisation. Here,
then, we have something like a clue to the phenomena—
phenomena which, as I have pointed out, are similar
and have much in common—of mesmeric sleep, of
hypnotism, and of electro-biology. We have already,
I hope, succeeded in eliminating from our minds the
false theory—the theory, that is to say, experimentally
proved to be false—that the will, or the gestures, or
the magnetic or vital fluid of the operator are necessary for the abolition of the consciousness and the
abeyance of the will of the subject. We now see
that ideas arising in the mind of the subject are sufficient to influence the circulation in the brain of the

person operated on, and such variations of the blood-supply of the brain as are adequate to produce sleep in the natural state or artificial slumber, either by total deprivation, or by excessive increase or local aberration in the quantity or quality of blood. In a like manner it is possible to produce coma and prolonged insensibility by pressure of the thumbs on the carotid ; or hallucinations, dreams, and visions by drugs, or by external stimulation of the nerves. Or again the consciousness may be only partially affected, and the person in whom sleep, coma or hallucination is produced, whether by physical means or by the influence of suggestion, may remain subject to the will of others and incapable of exercising his own volition.

Let me illustrate how easily the will may be abolished under the influence of imagination or of sudden impression, even in creatures the least imaginative and physically the most restless and active. Some very old experiments will suffice, though it is easy to modify them in new forms. I prefer the old, because the old story is one of ancient beginnings, of which we have now, however, the means of a more rational understanding. I take a cock, and I repeat on it what is known as the *experimentum mirabile* of Kircher. It is fresh from the barn-yard, and a very pugnacious animal. If I hold it, it struggles and screams ; but I have only to place it quietly and firmly on a board, and draw a chalk line from its beak, which I have depressed, until it touches the board, and the bird remains firmly

hypnotised, It is motionless, or, as people would say,
fascinated; and it will remain in this position for an
indefinite time. I take a rabbit and adjust it on its
back in a little trough, which is only used to prevent
it from falling over, and this animal also becomes
rapidly hypnotised. The same thing can be done with
a guinea-pig, a frog, or even with a young alligator.
The limbs are plastic, can be moved in any direction,
and will stay in the position in which they are placed.
The same thing can be done with a number of other
animals, such as birds and cray-fish. Harting states
that if this experiment be frequently repeated with
a fowl, the bird will often become permanently paralysed in some of its limbs. If I take up the hypnotised rabbit, or lift the cock, they at once become
active, and come out of their hypnotic into their natural
state. Position and tactile impression are the means
used in these experiments to produce hypnotism, and
possibly also mental impression. Visual impression
produces similar effects. Richet has with a lime-light
produced similar effects to those which Charcot produces on his hypnotic, cataleptic, and hysterical
patients. Horses are very susceptible to hypnotisation by any one standing in front of them, so that
they have to look at the operator fixedly. This practice was introduced into use in Austria by a cavalry
officer, Balassa. It is called after him the *Balassiren*
of horses, and according to Moll it has been introduced by law into Austria for the shoeing of horses

in the army. Rabbits, when they are introduced into the cage of a snake, fascinate themselves, as it is termed, by staring at it. The process is commonly spoken of as though it were an active proceeding on the part of the snake which fascinates the rabbits. They are, in fact, self-fascinated, and, as I pointed out in the case of hypnotic patients, a mechanical means of impressing their senses suffices, and it is quite gratuitous to import the notion of any sort of vital force or living influence of fascination on the part either of the snake or of the wily platform performer.

I now come to consider the subsequent conditions of the individual who has submitted to any of the processes of hypnotisation or mesmerism. They are sufficiently various, striking, and interesting, though they have been much misunderstood, considerably exaggerated, and the medium of much imposture. The individual is reduced more or less perfectly to the state of a living automaton. The upper brain is more or less completely and more or less regularly bloodless, and its functions are in abeyance. The will is abolished, suspended, or enfeebled. Sleep has been induced while the thought has been in relation to the person carrying on the experiment, and the suggestions made by, or the directions given by him are carried out without the intervention of the will of the subject and more or less completely without his knowledge. He may often be placed in positions which, in his waking moments, his terror or his reason would prevent him from taking up or from maintaining. The suggestions of attack or of defence, of causes of terror or of delight, are at once adopted, and he is as an instrument on the keys of which the operator can play his own tune. He accepts any statement as to flavours or odours; he swallows petroleum with delight, and believes it is champagne; mistakes salt for sugar, and mustard for honey. Of course, when all these tricks are played upon the platform, they are very far from always being genuine. A platform performance, in order to be successful in drawing money, must always have its dramatic and histrionic incidents. These desiderata cannot always be secured, and so confederates are paid to simulate the phenomena of hypnotism and suggestion; but there are few of the things done regularly at exhibitions of the kind which I have not seen repeated and surpassed from time to time in the study or the hospital ward. I refer to the works of Charcot, of Bernheim, of Moll, and of Déjérine for the details of marvellous effects of suggestion in producing, without the consciousness of the patient, antics, muscular efforts, contortions, perverted beliefs, bizarre actions which have had no counterpart in stage performances; but in the hands of the honest and capable men to whom I have referred they are all ascertained to be due to the influence of suggestion upon persons previously robbed of their will and thrown into the hypnotic state by any of the methods of physical or mental hypnotisation to which I have referred. It may be asked what are the added powers of clairvoyance, prediction of future events, insight into hidden things, and the development of new powers often attributed to somnambulists and hypnotics, and so frequently employed as a means of extorting money. The answer is given in one word—imposture—imposture—imposture! It is an imposture which has frequently recurred, and, though often exposed, is so lucrative and so attractive to the mystics and the so-called psychological researchers, that in one form or another it frequently revives.

In 1837 the French Academy appointed a commission to examine the marvels presented by blindfold subjects who had been submitted to what was called animal magnetism. All their pretensions were dissipated; there was neither magnetism nor any power of second sight. This report was disputed. Dr. Budin then offered a prize of 3,000 francs to any person, somnambulist or otherwise, who could read without the use of his eyes. Six candidates from different parts of France presented themselves, for animal magnetism and somnambulism were then epidemic. A new commission was appointed, new failures occurred. Trials went on until October 1840, when, at the close of a series of ignominious failures, in which the tricks of each pretender in succession were unmasked, the Academy decided that it would no longer take notice of any communications relative to the imposture and folly, miscalled animal magnetism and clairvoyance. The same thing occurred with Sir James Simpson, who twenty years afterwards, when similar pretences were rife in

the United Kingdom, and somnambulists and clairvoyants and thought-readers were again taking the
field, offered to present a 500*l*. note, which he had
locked in a box and placed in a bank, to anyone who
could read the number as the note lay in the box. It
was never claimed. Mr. Labouchere's similar experiment with the so-called thought-reader Bishop is of
quite recent date, but was performed under much less
rigid conditions, and by a person whose pretensions,
although they excited a great deal of attention, were
more than usually absurd.

Finally, let me refer to an aspect of the influence of
suggestion which, as a possible social danger, has engaged
the attention of lawyers and physicians—the influence
of deferred suggestion. It has been shown that not
only will a hypnotic subject perform unconsciously, under
the influence of suggestion, acts which are dangerous
to himself and others, and are in themselves criminal
—so that he can be made to thieve, to commit arson,
or to attempt violence—but that certain subjects
can, there is reason to believe, be made to receive a
suggestion having in it a time-element. He can be
told, 'On this day week, at a given time, you will
return to the hypnotic state, you will go to a given
place, you will steal such and such property, or you will
attack such and such a person, and you will not remember who gave you the direction.' These are extreme cases, and this is a surprising and dangerous
development of the influence of suggestion on the

trained and practised hypnotic—that is to say, on the person who has habitually surrendered his will and made himself the creature of another individual.

So complex is the brain as an organ of mind, that we cannot attempt to fully explain the mechanism of this operation; but there are facts within our ordinary knowledge which give some clue even to this pheno- menon. There is a time-element in all nerve actions and the operations of the brain. It is a very common thing for a person who puts himself to sleep at night to say to himself, ' I will wake at six o'clock to-morrow morning, for I have to catch a train.' This is a familiar example of a deferred suggestion operating at a moment indicated several hours before. In abnormal conditions of the nervous system, a shaking fit of ague will return at the same hour every third day or fourth day. The sensation of hunger is periodic according to the habit induced by the hour of eating. This periodic, chronometric and involuntary operation of the nervous system is imported into hypnotism. There are also other more complicated examples of time-element in the active and passive functions of the brain. There are the two or three well-observed and thoroughly authenticated instances in which persons have been found to live two different lives, with different mental characters and different capacities, at regular intervals in the course of the year; knowing nothing and re- membering nothing during the one period of what they were thinking or doing in the other. Which of these should be considered the normal state of brain circulation, and which the abnormal or hypnotic, it would be difficult to determine; but to recall these facts suffices to indicate that the introduction of the time-element in deferred suggestion has nothing of the supernatural, implies no conferring of new powers on the individual, and is only the introduction into advanced and highly developed stages of hypnotism of a functional action which is more or less natural with all brains. The only other examples to which I need refer of the attempt to import into the subjective phenomena described the element of the supernatural and the discovery of an unknown force are the so-called spiritualists and the telepathists. Their pretensions are only a revival under a new form of the old follies and deceptions—often self-deceptions, and still more often impostures—which surrounded the earlier introductions of the errors of the magnetisers, the spiritualists, and the mesmerists of the middle ages. The second-sight and clairvoyance of the witches and the demoniacs, of the mystics and the mesmerists, having been exposed and discredited, the same things are still from time to time revived under new names more suited to a generation which has got rid of some of the nomenclature of the past. Telepathy sounds better to modern ears than mesmeric trance or clairvoyance, but it has no more substantial foundation. It is an attempt to discover whether it is possible to see without eyes, to hear without ears, to receive or convey impressions without the aid of the special senses. The spirit-rappers, the Davenports, the Bishops, the thought-readers, the animal magnetisers, have dropped into darkness, and are buried in oblivion. Telepathy is a silly attempt to revive in a pseudo-scientific form such as self-deception of this kind has always assumed, but in a very feeble form, and with very futile and inane results, the failures and impostures of the past. Happily, the belief in telepathy is confined to a few, and those, I am ashamed to say, chiefly in this country. It has had a feeble and lingering existence, and is undoubtedly destined to die a premature death.

To conclude: these delusions, this miracle-monger-ing, these disordered visions and hysteric hallucina-tions, this exploitation of the love of the mysterious, these pseudo-magnetic attractions, these sham scientific floatings in the air or fixations of the body, these thought-readings and foretellings, these vain pronounce-ments concerning unseen worlds and invisible planes of being, these playings on the fears, the hopes, the feeble senses, the eager imaginations, and the ill-balanced reason of the masses, are as old as, nay, apparently older than history. Sometimes in this, as in other things, we are tempted to ask, 'Does the world make any progress, or are we still moving on the same planes and in the same grooves of ignorance and superstition, knavery, folly, and self-deception?' I think we may find comfort, however, in the historical review. It is true that we have still with us the spiritists, the stage hypnotists, the living magnets, the Mahatmas, the belated psychical researchers, and the ghost seers. But they are only the stunted remnants, the vestigial and atrophied traces indicating the later stages of ages of development, in which we have outgrown the period when such follies and fallacies were the almost universal heritage of mankind, and led to burnings, drownings, torture, and wholesale misery, when the cataleptics and hypnotics were counted by thousands and sometimes by hundreds of thousands at a time, when imposture was widespread and high-placed, when philosophers were the dupes of their own self-deception, and when the mischiefs of hypnotic suggestion were extended over large districts and sapped the reason and ruined the lives of thousands. There are still performances and publications which in their follies and their capacities for mischief rival some of those prevalent in the darkest periods of ignorance and superstition, but they are at the present time regarded as curiosities and eccentricities, and provoke laughter and derision where formerly they would have led to insanity and persecution.

HYPNOTISM, ANIMAL MAGNETISM, AND HYSTERIA [1]

THE MAGNET IN MEDICINE

THE remarkable properties of the natural magnet, its capacity for action without contact, and the respective attracting and repelling powers of its two poles, have greatly impressed the imagination of mankind from a very early date; and, as Richer,[2] Binet, and Féré have pointed out, the assumption that the magnet possessed some mysterious influence on the body, capable of being turned to account in the cure of disease, was prevalent in the Middle Ages. Magnetic rings were worn to cure nervous diseases, and the electrotherapeutic frauds, follies, and delusions which are so rampant in the present day can boast a very ancient history of trickery, credulity and folly. Electric rings, belts, and boxes were hung round the body in the time of Cædon. Paracelsus characteristically taught ' that the human body was endowed with a double magnetism—that one

[1] Reprinted from the *British Medical Journal*.
[2] Richer, *Bulletin de la Société de Biologie*, May 30th, 1884. Paul Richer, *Nouvelle Revue*, August 1st, 1882. Binet and Féré *Animal Magnetism*, 1888.

portion attracted to itself the planets, and was nourished
by them, whence came wisdom, thought, and the senses;
that the other portion attracted to itself the elements,
and disintegrated them, whence came flesh and blood;
that the attractive and hidden virtue of man resembles
those of amber and of the magnet, and that by this
virtue the magnetic virtue of healthy persons attracts
the enfeebled magnetism of those who are sick.'

MESMER AND HIS DUPES

Mesmer, who gives his name to the practice called
mesmerism, did not think it sufficient to use talismans
and magic boxes, but introduced contact and passes
with the hand by which to communicate what he called
the magnetic virtue due to animal magnetism. He declared that by this method 'the physician may judge
with certainty of the origin, nature, and progress of
diseases, however complicated they be; he may hinder
their development and accomplish their cure without exposing the patient to dangerous and troublesome consequences, irrespective of age, temperament
and sex. Even women in a state of pregnancy and
during parturition may reap the same advantages.'

I have already spoken elsewhere [1] of the immense
popularity achieved by Mesmer's practices, and of his
mesmeric *baquets* or troughs filled with bottles of water
and iron filings, around which stood rows of patients hold-

---

[1] *Nineteenth Century*, 1891, and p. 8.

ing iron rods issuing from the troughs, the subjects being tied to each other by cords and joining hands. Perfect silence was maintained, soft music was heard, and remarkable effects were obtained. Some patients were convulsed, and had to be taken away to a padded room, against the walls of which they might knock their heads without injury; others were thrown into a state of semi-stupor, or, in the language of to-day, into a hypnotic state, in which they were submissive to the master, and from which his voice or look could arouse them. Some patients became affectionate and embraced each other, others fell into fits of immoderate laughter, shrieking, or tears. The convulsive agitation frequently lasted for hours, and according to the account of an eye-witness (Bailly), these symptoms were preceded or followed by a state of languor or dreaminess, by a species of depression and even by stupor. I quote from Binet and Féré the following graphic account of the proceedings :

Mesmer, wearing a coat of lilac silk, walked up and down amid this agitated crowd in company with Deslon and his associates, whom he chose for their youth and comeliness. Mesmer carried a long iron wand, with which he touched the bodies of the patients, and especially the diseased parts. Often laying aside the wand, he magnetised the patients with his eyes, fixing his gaze on theirs, or applying his hands to the hypochondriac region and to the lower part of the abdomen. This application was often continued for hours, and at other times the master made use of passes. He began by placing himself *en rapport* with his subject.   Seated opposite to him, foot against foot, knee against knee, Mesmer laid his fingers on the hypochondriac region and moved them to and fro, lightly touching the ribs.   Magnetisation with strong currents was substituted for these manipulations when more energetic results were to be produced.   The master, raising his fingers in a pyramidal form, passed his hands all over the patient's body, beginning with the head, and going downwards over the shoulders to the feet.   He then returned to the head, both back and front, to the belly and the back, and renewed the process again and again until the magnetised person was saturated with the healing fluid, and transported with pain or pleasure, both sensations being equally salutary.[1]   Young women were so much gratified by the 'crisis' that they begged to be thrown into it anew ; they followed Mesmer through the hall, and confessed that it was impossible not to be warmly attached to the person of the magnetiser.

THE 'POSSESSED' AND THE 'DEMONIACS'

The inference drawn by eyewitnesses and by the subjects of these practices was that 'it is impossible not to admit from all these results that some great force acts upon and masters the patient, and that this force appears to reside in the magnetiser.'   Now these conditions and practices will, no doubt, at once be seen to have a very close resemblance and an obvious relation to what may be read in the records of possessed persons—or 'demoniacs' as they were called in the Middle Ages—who play so prominent a part in cer-

Louis Figuier, *Histoire du Merveilleux*, vol. ii. p. 20.   Paris : 1860.

tain phases of history, and in scenes which have been pictorially depicted by some of the great masters of Italy, Flanders, and France, from the fifteenth to the seventeenth centuries.[1] Their pictures of striking and historic scenes of this kind represent phenomena attested by a mass of the most undoubted evidence. It is not the facts of which we need entertain any doubt; it is only of the interpretation of them that we shall be able to afford a more modern version. To Professor Charcot and his pupils—prominent among whom are Richer, Babinsky, Bourneville, and Féré—we are indebted for a long series of masterly, laborious, and original researches on the subject of hypnotism, its near relative hysteria and the whole chain of conditions belonging to the family of hypnotism. Professor Charcot's luminous researches are epoch-making in this department of knowledge, and his extensive collection of photographic reproductions of hypnotic and hypno-hysteric patients is replete with treasures of nerve aberrations.

The Key to the Phenomena Subjective and Resident in the Patient

It will, no doubt, readily occur to the minds of those who are at all versed in the scenes now witnessed from time to time that the occurrences, so vividly represented in the pictures already referred to, and

[1] See Richer's *Les Démoniaques dans l'Art.*

those described as occurring among the patients of
Mesmer under the influence of holding the iron rods
attached to his bottles and iron filings, are from time
to time reproduced in these our modern days on the
platform of the hypnotist, by the faith-curer, and
amongst the pilgrims to Lourdes. But as we are less
apt to speak now of demoniacs and possessed, these
phenomena are usually characterised by words selected
from a pseudo-scientific and not from the theological
vocabulary. I may say at once that I am now leading
up to the demonstration that the conditions induced,
whether of convulsion, cataleptic immobility, languor,
submissiveness, trance or acceptance of suggestion and
command, may be shown to be due to a nervous condition or mental state arising in the individual subject
either from physical or mental excitation; and further
that such conditions, by whatever distinctive names their
varieties may be called, are not and never were due
to any healing power or to any fluid or magnetic influence or mesmeric or hypnotic power resident in the
operator. It is a common delusion that the mesmerist
or hypnotiser counts for anything in the experiment.
The operator, whether priest, physician, charlatan, self-
deluded enthusiast or conscious impostor, is not the
source of any occult influence, does not possess any
mysterious power, and plays only a very secondary
and insignificant part in the chain of phenomena observed. There exist at the present time many individuals who claim for themselves, and some who

make a living by so doing, a peculiar property or power as potent mesmerisers, hypnotisers, magnetisers, or electro-biologists. One even often hears it said in society (for I am sorry to say that these mischievous practices and pranks are sometimes made a society game) that such a person is a clever hypnotist or has great mesmeric or healing power. I hope to be able to prove what I firmly hold, both from my own personal experience and experiment, as I have already related in the *Nineteenth Century* that there is no such thing as a potent mesmeric influence, no such power resident in any one person more than another; that a glass of water, a tree, a stick, a penny-post letter, or a limelight can mesmerise as effectually as can any individual. A clever hypnotiser means only a person who is acquainted with the physical or mental tricks by which the hypnotic condition is produced; or sometimes an unconscious impostor who is unaware of the very trifling part for which he is cast in the play, and who supposes himself really to possess a mysterious power which in fact he does not possess at all, or which, to speak more accurately, is equally possessed by every stock or stone.

HYPNOTISM AND HYSTERIA CONDITIONS OF DISTURBED EQUILIBRIUM

The condition of hypnotism, mesmerism, &c., is a mental condition—a condition of disturbed equilibrium of the nervous system and brain apparatus of the person operated on. With that key to unlock this curious cabinet of mysteries, delusions, and veritable phenomena, we shall be able the more easily to understand the interpolated illustrations of hypnotic and pseudo-hypnotic patients and conditions. They represent patients in the Salpêtrière Hospital who present all the conditions usually spoken of as due to the mysterious power of the hypnotiser or the mesmerist, and associated with the exercise of some mysterious influence by that sinister personage, by his command of the imaginary fluid, magnetic, electric or telepathic, supposed to issue from his finger ends, or to emanate from his body. These phenomena are the induction of sleep or partial sleep, of cataleptic lethargy, of the loss or temporary abolition of ordinary sensation, of incapacity for feeling pain on being pricked or cut, and of loss of taste, so that neither pepper, salt nor any nauseous substance produces any impression on the palate, and any one substance may at the suggestion of the operator be mistaken for any other, as paraffin for champagne, salt for sugar, cayenne pepper for sweetmeats.

The Identity of Phenomena in Hysteria and Hypnotic Suggestion

Everyone knows something about hysteria. Everyone is acquainted with that ordinary form of hysteria which is characterised frequently by what is known

as an hysterical fit, and is accompanied by temporary
convulsions often not distinguishable from epileptic
convulsions, except that the patient, although unconscious, may generally be trusted not to hurt her or
himself. Hysterical patients rarely or never bite their
tongue as epileptics generally do, but they go through
violent contortions, show evidences of various uncon-
trolled emotions, the fit, whether lasting for a short
or a long time, commonly ending in languor, or a long
sleep and perhaps a flood of tears. Here already some
resemblance to the hypnotic state and to the condition
of convulsionists and demoniacs is apparent. Medical
men know, however, and many others have become
acquainted incidentally with the fact, that these attacks
when of a severe character or in highly nervous and
unstable individuals may go much further, and some
striking illustrations of most of the phenomena characteristic of the extreme degrees of hypnotisation and
suggestibility, without the employment of any hypnotic
influences and arising only out of the disturbed equilibrium of the nervous system of the patient herself or
himself, are here illustrated. I say herself or himself,
because hysteria, even in its most highly-developed
eccentric and extreme forms, is by no means the exclusive privilege of the female sex, although it is their
more general attribute.

SELF-SUGGESTED EMOTIONS AND ATTITUDES OF HYSTERICS

Fig. 1 shows a person in a state of what is not hysterical lethargy spontaneously arising in a hysterical patient, but hypnotic lethargy artificially induced. Fig. 2 is a photograph of a female hysteric seized with an attack in which her body is arched in a tetanic spasm, unconscious, and the whole weight of the body in this violently constrained position supported for a length of time by the head and heels. In fig. 3 we return to artificially induced hypnotic condition. The patient will stay in the position represented, into which she can be thrown artificially by a strong light or a loud sound, or by being made to stare at any fixed object for an almost indefinite length of time. If the most delicate form of register be attached to her uplifted arm, it will be found that there is no tremor or unconscious muscular movement, which is not the case with an impostor or with anyone voluntarily assuming this posture for any length of time.

To these are added some of the emotional phases and phenomena of hysteria. Fig. 4 is a characteristic picture of hysterical delirium ; fig. 5 of an hysterical patient who, in the course of her attack, is under the influence of pleasing impressions; fig. 6, the same patient under a similar self-suggested emotion of anger ; fig. 7 shows an hysterical patient who is subject to strong religious impressions, and in one of the periods of her attack falls into the position of crucifixion.

FIG. 1.

FIG. 2.

FIG. 3.

FIG. 4.

FIG. 5.

FIG. 6.

E

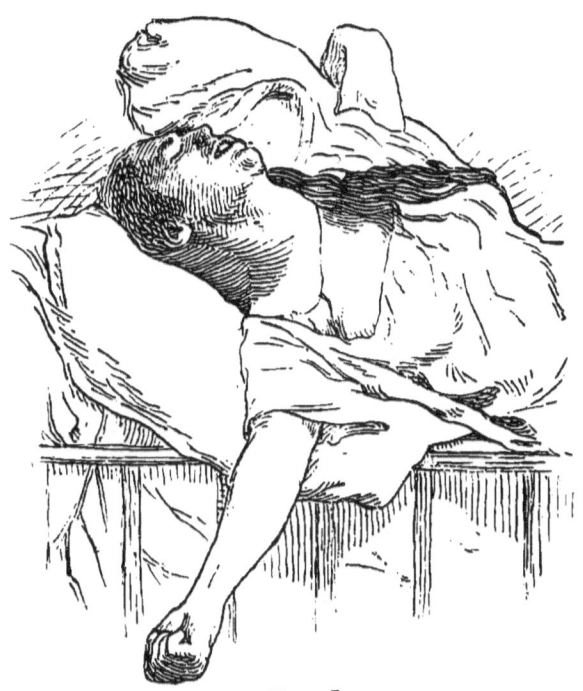

FIG. 7.

Similar Conditions Induced in Hypnotics by Suggestion, Auto-suggestion, and Physical Impressions

I now illustrate the artificially-induced hypnotic state, and show how our hypnotic patient is subject to the influence of impulses conveyed to her mind either by the voice of the operator or by self-generated influence in the brain, due to such simple conditions as the position of her muscles and the nature of the attitude in which she is placed. She has already been illustrated in the attitude of fixed and what is called 'cataleptic' immobility; but her hands being raised into the attitude of astonishment (fig. 8), the change of expression in the face should be noted as indicating that the change of muscular attitude and the influence of the associated muscular action, related habitually to the emotion of astonishment, have produced that emotion in her mind and it is strikingly depicted in her face. In fig. 9 her fists have been doubled, and she has been placed in a fighting attitude. In fig. 10 her hands are placed in the position in which women, and especially Frenchwomen, are in the habit of going through the little performance called 'throwing a kiss.' Few actresses, I imagine, however able, accomplished, and remarkable for histrionic power and intelligence, could so rapidly assume and maintain the unaffected expression of graceful welcome such as this unconscious and uneducated woman has assumed under the impulse of a brain emotion generated by the simple impulse of associated muscular influence in the related brain centres, unrestrained by the self-consciousness which so often spoils the best acting. Self-consciousness is, in virtue of her condition, completely abolished. She is a mere puppet, the slave of unconscious cerebration excited by external influences and suggestion, or of the suggestion of her own muscles.

Another example of the influence of mere physical suggestion may be studied in fig. 11, a girl in the attitude of prayer. Note the intensity of her imploring expression, which might serve as a study for a painter ; the idea of prayer has not been suggested to her by word of mouth, nor is this the self-suggestion of a hysteric ; it is the attitude induced, and always induced in this particular patient, when hypnotised by the sudden influence of a strong light thrown through the medium of blue glass. The same girl is always dazed and thrown into the hypnotic state under the influence of a strong yellow light. Not only, however, does the whole body of the hypnotised patient or of the highly hysteric patient lend itself thus easily to the influence of physical excitation or suggestion from without, or of ideas aroused by the action of local groups of muscles or of other physical excitations within the body, but individual muscles can just as easily be acted on and separately set in motion. The mere stroking of the extensor muscles of one or two fingers

FIG. 8.

FIG. 9.

FIG. 10.

FIG. 11.

will throw them into extension, while the touching of any set of flexor muscles will produce violent contraction and extreme flexion of the limb.

I hope I have made it sufficiently clear that there are a number of conditions, either spontaneous or artificially produced, in which, while the power of will is abolished, and the brain loses its restraining and controlling power, emotions may be excited, feelings induced, and intellectual operations set in motion, independently of the will of the individual, and without individual consciousness being alive to what is going on. I have endeavoured to show that all these various and allied conditions may and do occur under several sets of circumstances and influences which at first sight seem very dissimilar, but (and this is the central point of my argument) are in reality related by a common bond. The convulsionists and the demoniacs were thrown into strange conditions of excitement, delusion, insensibility to pain and hallucination under the influence of the sight of similar conditions in others or of suggestion by word of mouth, and they became amenable to and were cured by the same agencies.

The Key to the Mystery

The key to all these phenomena was first given by our countryman, Mr. James Braid, of Manchester, in 1840-50. His explanation is exceedingly well stated in his admirable little pamphlet entitled ' Magic, Witchcraft, Animal Magnetism, Hypnotism, and Electro-Biology,' of which the third edition was published by Churchill, in 1852. It was Braid who first introduced the appropriate word, hypnotism, to describe these phenomena. He showed that the effects of the hypnotist are produced by setting in motion certain ideas in the mind of the individual, that the individual always hypnotises himself, and that hypnotism is a state of induced sleep produced by verbal suggestion or by artificial contrivance.

I may add that in repeating over and over again these experiments I have confirmed Braid's results, and have further proved that the will of the operator has nothing whatever to do with inducing sleep in the patient. You may, in operating after the varied methods of the mesmerist, the hypnotist, or the electro-biologist, will that the patient shall do whatever you please—sleep or not sleep, but your will, unless it is expressed or indicated to the patient so as to afford him a mental suggestion on which he unconsciously acts, will count for nothing ; he will fall into hypnotic sleep. His condition depends on what he thinks you wish and not on what you really wish ; and if you set before him a glass of water or a penny-post letter, or put him in front of a tree or a candle, and tell him that you have mesmerised it, and order him to look at it and to be influenced by it, he will be influenced by it whether you have made any passes over it or not, whether you have magnetised it or not, and whether you wish it

to influence him or not.   You have, in fact, very little
to do with the matter as the operator, except in so far
as you influence by your suggestion, and by the subject's conception of your will, his nervous system and
his state of mind.

Verbally Expressed or Physical Impressions only are Capable of Conveying Suggestions

In the same way, when once the subject is thoroughly
hypnotised the operator can do nothing with him by
willing or by wishing unless he express to him in
words, or indicate to him by some other method capable
of physically conveying to him a suggestion, what he
wishes him to do or what the subject thinks the operator
wishes him to do.   Any physical excitation may in this
hypnotic state excite physical changes, as I have shown,
in his muscular or nervous system, which will in their
turn give rise in the subject to mental emotion, to
hallucinations, or to self-generated acts of the strangest
kind.   So largely is his restraining brain power put to
sleep, and for the time abolished, so largely is his intelligent consciousness held in abeyance, that he becomes
a marvellous machine, astonishingly, blindly, actively
obedient to the wildest orders or the most *bizarre* suggestions.   He can be made to believe himself a cat, a dog,
a lion, a rat, and to act accordingly, so far as a human
machine can act.   His intelligent consciousness of
impressions conveyed by the nerves of common sensa-

tion or of special sense has been abolished; his skin may be pierced with needles and he will not feel it; mustard or salt or assafœtida may be placed on his tongue, and he will either not taste them or mistake them for anything the operator pleases to name, and he will testify the most genuine and ludicrous dislike of or most intense disgust at the substance placed in his mouth. The operator can induce sentiments of anger, nay, even of violent and destructive rage, ecstasy, affection or grief, at will, by verbal suggestions. He has, in fact, under his hands a marvellous and God-created machine, abased and degraded by the abolition of intelligence and self-restraint.

THE CONDITION PURELY SUBJECTIVE: ANYONE OR ANYTHING CAN HYPNOTISE

To produce these effects there is no cleverness wanted on the part of the hypnotiser, there is no special power in this matter resident in him; anyone can hypnotise and everyone can hypnotise if he is patient enough, and either scientifically intelligent or ignorantly fanatic. The marvel and the mystery is in the individual operated upon. What is the precise nature of this complex and astonishing mechanism of body and mind which binds together, in such singular complexity of relation, muscle and nerve, lower brain, upper brain, nerves of special sense, body and viscera, no anatomist, however accomplished, no physiologist, however learned or acute, can explain. We have before us only the wonderful facts, and they are far more wonderful than any of the sham tricks of the clairvoyant, the mesmerist, or the magnetist who plays upon them and uses them for his purpose of imposture, self-deception, or of vain mystery-mongering.

The Therapeutic Uselessness and Social Mischief of Hypnotism

Can these facts be put to any good use? Of this I am bound to say there is no present evidence except with relation to the most insignificant and imperfect results, and in my opinion there is little prospect of any. Esdaile showed long ago that the anæsthesia induced by hypnotism can be employed for the purposes of surgical operation, but the process is so tedious, the duration of anæsthesia so uncertain, and the number of persons whose nervous system is in the unstable condition which makes them amenable to hypnotic influence happily so few, that as a practical method of anæsthesia it is unavailable, and far inferior to the chemical action of chloroform and other narcotic vapours. The same holds good of hypnotism as an ordinary hypnotic. It is far less certain, far more troublesome, much more rarely capable of application, and much more likely to produce mischief, than opium or sulphonal, or any other of a dozen narcotics which are always at hand, are cheap, easily used and under ordinary circumstances innocuous when properly administered.

As to the treatment of other diseases, I have, I believe, read all that is to be read on the subject, whether from the schools of Nancy, Paris, or Vienna, and I have arrived at the conclusion that Professor Charcot, with his abundant good sense, his great erudition, and his vast experience, is fully justified in the conclusion at which he and his eminent pupils, Richer, Babinsky, Déjerine and others have arrived; that for curative purposes hypnotism is very rarely useful, generally entirely useless, and often injurious.

The Practice of Hypnotism, except by Skilled Physicians, should be Forbidden

And here I will end by saying that, since no evident advantage has during forty years of extensive, patient and elaborate trial and research been obtainable by the hundreds of physicians and physiologists who have devoted themselves to the study of the question, it is therefore justifiable to conclude that the practice of hypnotism, mesmerism, electro-biology, and so-called animal magnetism, being almost invariably useless and often dangerous, even in the hands of the most highly skilled, careful and conscientious physicians, is a practice which ought to be forbidden to the unqualified, and is most unfit and improper for platform performances. It is equally unsuited for private amusement and is dangerous and improper as a society game. It is liable to gross abuse, and is frequently the means of fraud and imposture, extortion of money, and degradation of body and mind, and is apt to induce serious injuries to both. The confirmed and trained hypnotic subject is a maimed individual in mind and body, and is likely at any time to be dangerous to himself and to society. Instances of these results are so common that I need not follow up this branch of the subject. I conclude by expressing the hope that this outline of the physical facts connected with hypnotic phenomena may help to arm those who have not previously had an opportunity of investigating the subject against the wiles of the impostor and the false suggestions of the somewhat profane persons who endeavour to connect these phenomena with the incarnation of spiritual power and relations in themselves or their favourite 'Sludge.' At any rate, I venture to hope that it may have given some correct ideas of the nature of the hypnotic state, and have cleared away some of the fictions which have been associated with it by imaginative, ill-informed, or interested persons.

MESMERISM
AND THE NEW WITCHCRAFT

The Forgotten Impostors—The Scientific Studies of Braid, and of Charcot and his School—Experiments and Publications of the author on Mesmerism, Hypnotism, and Hysteria—The Rational Interpretation of the Veritable Facts—Hypnotism, a Subjective Phenomenon—The Marvels of La Charité and of the École Polytechnique—Reports of British Journalists thereon—The Subjects of Demonstration—Definition and Preliminary Phenomena of Hypnotisation: Their Dangers—Methods of Inducing Sleep—'Magnetic' Susceptibility and Perceptions—Blue Flames and Red—Attraction and Repulsion—Magnetised Photographs and Engravings—Stored-up Thoughts in a Magnetic Band—Psychical Phenomena—Influence of Drugs in Tubes applied to the Neck—Drunkenness without Drink—A Human Cat—Dr. Luys's Demonstration—The Control Experiments—Dr. Luys's Recent Declaration that his Subjects were Unworthy of Confidence—The Moral Dilemma—Appeal to Dr. Luys for Explanations—Details of Experiments with False Magnets and Misnamed Medicinal Tubes—Results of the Control—Some Counter-Experiments—Evidence of Drs. De Cyon, Louis Olivier, and Lutaud—Fact and Fiction in Hypnotism—Hysteria at the Salpêtrière and Hypnotism at La Charité—Dr. Luys's Testimony to the Dangers of Hypnotism—Letter from a Trained Subject—Hypnotism and the New Magic—The Library of Marvels—A Modern Sorceress—Evidence of Charcot and Babinski—Medical Uses of Hypnotism Limited to Manifestations of Hysteria—Its Frequent Failures even in that Domain—Valueless in the Treatment of Mental Disease (Magnan, Forel, Briand)—Hypnotism before the Courts of Law—Inapplicable

*to Surgery or Obstetrics—Essential Identity of Faith-Cures
and Hypnotic Cures—Summary—The Relative Success of the
Faith-Cures of the Laboratory, the Chapel, and the Grotto.*

I HAVE been spending Christmas week and the early
days of the new year in the ' Pays des Merveilles.'   For
scenic effects and thaumaturgical performances the
wards of Dr. Luys, membre de l'Académie de Médecine,
at the Hôpital de la Charité, surpass those to which we
have all been more or less accustomed at the theatres of
magic and the conjurers' halls on the boulevards of
Paris or in Piccadilly.   Ordinary hypnotic performances
have still enough attraction to draw large audiences in
the provinces, but they are growing somewhat stale and
out of fashion in the metropolitan centres.   The spiritual-
istic tricks of the Davenport Brothers, the reading of
names and dates in sealed envelopes, and the appearance of corresponding writings on the arms of mediums
such as Foster, the materialisation of flowers and
diamond rings out of space, the externalisation of the
' spirit form ' of mediums as in the case of Katie King,
the slate-writing of Slade, the levitation of Hume, the
reinforcement of muscular strength of the Georgian
Magnet, have all had their day of sham mystery, of
pseudo-marvel and of profitable exploitation.   They
have in turn retreated into the shadow of obscurity
and oblivion, or passed to the platform of other conjurers who ' show how it is done.'   But the love of
mystery and the pursuit of the unknown are durable
elements in what, in order to be quite modern, must

perhaps be termed the psychology of mankind, and 'the public' still clamour to be deceived.

Recently attention has been attracted anew to the phenomena which have been known and described in one form or other for centuries under the titles of fascination, mesmerism, animal magnetism, and hypnotism, phenomena which were for the first time intelligently investigated and rationally explained by our countryman Braid. Since the time of Braid little or nothing had been added to our knowledge of the phenomena in question until Professor Charcot thoroughly studied the subject at the Salpêtrière Hospital, convinced himself of the identity of the hypnotic susceptibility with the condition of hysteria in men and women, and worked upon those lines.

The long-continued studies of Charcot, and of his pupils Binet, Féré, Déjérine, Richer, Bourneville, Babinski and Ballet, and the continuous and much frequented public demonstrations at the Salpêtrière Hospital, naturally attracted great attention to the subject. These studies and demonstrations have helped materially to define and classify the forms and stages of the hypnotic and hysteric conditions.

In a lecture which I gave at Toynbee Hall, and which constitutes the first chapter of this book, I published for the first time the results of a series of experiments and observations made by me from time to time during the last thirty years on the facts and follies of mesmerism and hypnotism. These in-

vestigations had convinced me, after the employment
of rigid test experiments and methods of control,
that the familiar and now well-known phenomena
of the hypnotic state are due to purely subjective
conditions; that there is no fluid of any sort and no
influence of any sort, tangible or intangible, which
passes in these cases from the operator to the subject,
except a suggestion by word of mouth or visible indications, and that it is quite sufficient that the subject
should have the belief that will is being exercised in
order that the acts should be performed and the conditions induced which are supposed to be the result
of a transferred influence or an unexpressed will.   I
have repeatedly ascertained by test experiments, which
anyone can repeat, that the will or the 'emanations'
from the person of the operator, so often invoked as
causatives, have nothing essentially to do with the
induced conditions in the hypnotic subject.   I have
ascertained by repeated experiments that the making
of passes is a senseless and unnecessary mummery,
unless it be done to impress the imagination, and that
the introduction of magnets, near or distant, has no real
relation to the induced conditions.   The sound of a
gong or the light of a wax candle, or of a limelight,
or an electric light, the striking of notes on a piano-
forte, the vibrations of a tuning-fork, a look, or a word,
the gazing at any bright object such as a metal spoon
or a coin, or the mere belief, however false and contrary to the fact, that an external influence is being

exercised, have in my experience sufficed to produce
in what are called susceptible subjects partial or profound sleep, catalepsy, somnambulism, lethargy, or
lucid slumber, and to reduce the subject to a condition of more or less complete automatism. In the
more recent lecture on 'Mesmerism, Hypnotism, and
Hysteria,' which precedes this paper, I have aimed at
showing, and as I believe have shown, how closely these
results to which my experiments had long since led
me are in accord with the carefully observed facts
and elaborate conclusions of Professor Charcot and
his school, and I have illustrated by photographs the
identity of the phenomena of hypnotism with those of
hysteria.

I had of course read for some years past from time
to time the statements and publications of a certain
school of writers, chiefly French, of whom the most
notable is Dr. Luys, physician to La Charité Hospital.
I also had the opportunity of seeing a quaint series
of experiments carried out some years ago by Dr.
Dumontpallier at La Pitié Hospital, which impressed
me only as indicating a surprising credulity and a still
more surprising ignorance or neglect of the ordinary
phenomena of hysteria. The published lectures and
reported demonstrations of Dr. Luys involved so many
extravagances and such singular conclusions that I had
purposely abstained from going to witness the performances. It was obviously difficult to test them impartially and independently, and it might have been hoped

that they would in the end prove innocuous by reason
of their extravagance, and would not seriously affect
the mind of any large portion of the intelligent public
in Paris, as they certainly had not had any success in
influencing medical opinion in this country.   Shortly
before my going to Paris, however, in response to an
official invitation to the Pasteur Jubilee, there appeared
in the 'Pall Mall Gazette' of December 2 and 15 two
articles headed ' Hypnotisers and Hypnotised in Paris,'
in which were picturesquely described, and vouched for
in evident good faith, performances of an astounding
character in the wards of La Charité and at the École
Polytechnique by a gentleman of considerable attain-
ments, I believe, in physical science, and of undoubted
sincerity.   Other articles in the London journals,
and in particular two communications on 'The New
Mesmerism' in the 'Times,' gave almost simultaneously
still greater prominence to these performances. I deter-
mined, therefore, to take the opportunity of witnessing
these demonstrations and of learning whatever there
might be new and capable of verification in this series
of experiments. They carried the pretensions of the
magnetist and the hypnotiser much further in certain
directions than had ever before been claimed by serious
experimenters in modern times. Moreover and especially, these demonstrations were alleged to be of the
nature of scientific and physical experiment, therefore
capable of control and test, which is very often not the
case where the phenomena presented pretend only to

be the result of new mental endowments, sharpened and enlarged intellectual perceptions, or the transference of ideas and thoughts by contact or ' through space.'

The reports of the Psychical Research Society of Great Britain have given only such crude results and inchoate conclusions, that they had never inspired me with much desire to test what I venture to consider the singularly inadequate and even puerile demonstrations which they professed to afford of telepathy and thought transference. But here the existence of broad, strongly marked and palpable results were averred which, if they bore the test of experiment, as it was declared they did, would prove nearly conclusive. On my way to Paris I met a medical friend, Dr. Lutaud, formerly resident in London, now a hospital physician in Paris, and editor of the ' Journal de Médecine,' who undertook to communicate with Dr. Luys, and to ask whether he would be willing to give me a demonstration of his experiments of thought transference, transference of sensibility, externalisation of sensation, influence of medicines in sealed tubes, &c., and of his results, also whether I could see the much-vaunted experiments of Colonel de Rochas d'Aiglun. The occasional correspondent of the ' Times ' had expressly declared that they were conducted in the wards of the hospital under circumstances which put imposture out of the question. I received in due time a communication from Dr. Lutaud, informing me that Dr. Luys would be at the hospital on the following morning and would afford

me the desired demonstration, and that he had further
invited Colonel de Rochas to be present and to demonstrate the results at which he had arrived.

Before beginning the narrative of what I saw and of
the subsequent steps which I took to verify the causation
and to investigate the meaning of these performances,
it may be as well to give extracts from these articles,
which created a widespread and deep impression on the
public mind, in order to explain what it was that I
' went out to see.'

EXTRACT FROM THE 'PALL MALL GAZETTE' OF
DECEMBER 2, 1892.

' Dr. Luys then showed me how a similar artificial state
of suffering could be created without suggestion—in fact,
by the mere proximity of certain substances. A pinch of
coal dust, for example, corked and sealed in a small phial,
and placed by the side of the neck of a hypnotised person,
produces symptoms of suffocation by smoke ; a tube of distilled water, similarly placed, provokes signs of incipient
hydrophobia ; while another very simple concoction put in
contact with the flesh brings on symptoms of suffocation by
drowning.   The intense congestion that these artificial
attacks produce might determine the rupture of a blood
vessel or the stoppage of the heart ; it is, therefore, unwise
to describe the experiments more fully lest anybody should
be tempted to try them without proper precautions.   But
there was an experiment of this nature that should be described, for it serves as a *trait d'union* that will enable me
to go from experimental to practical hypnotism.   The
woman who had been hypnotised earlier in the morning
was put to sleep for a second time, and a corked and sealed

tube containing 15 grains of brandy was put in contact
with her neck. A few seconds later she commenced to
make grimaces, and moved her tongue and lips as if she
were tasting liquor of some kind. She then began talking
in broken phrases : " I'm thirsty ; I want something to
drink ; give me something to drink ; my head pains me so ;
anyone would say I was drunk." She tried to stand on her
feet, and fell heavily down into a chair. " There," said Dr.
Luys, who had previously taken his visitors out of the
room to explain what would happen on contact of the tube
containing alcohol with the hypnotised person, " now, a
strange thing is that this artificial state of drunkenness
can be transferred to another hypnotised person."

'A man was brought in from an adjoining room and
hypnotised. One of his hands was placed in the hand of
the woman, and the passage of a magnet along their arms
in the direction of the man sufficed to transfer the symptoms
of drunkenness to him. To all appearances he was quite
as drunk as the woman seemed to have been a few moments
earlier. The transfer of disease to hypnotised subjects is
one of the most frequent methods of cure adopted by the
doctors in charge of the Clinique Hypnothérapique of the
Charité. It is not every patient that can be hypnotised
and submitted to a course of treatment by suggestion, so
this alternative way of profiting by hypnotic methods is in
vogue.'

EXTRACT FROM THE 'PALL MALL GAZETTE,'
DECEMBER 15, 1892.

'I was led to study the exteriorisation of the sensitiveness
in this way, and it was the merest chance that it happened.
One day it happened that I hypnotised a subject on a velvet-
backed chair in my office. The subject was taken across the
room, and when she was seated at some distance from the

chair I accidentally touched the velvet, and, to my surprise, the woman put her hand to her back and showed signs of intense suffering. It was evident that the earlier contact of the subject and the chair had charged the latter in some way. I then tried with a silk-covered chair, but the same result was not produced. Still, the first observation satisfied me that not only was it possible to exteriorise the sensitiveness of a human being, but that the sensitiveness could be stored up in some other substance. At the Hôpital de la Charité you have yourself seen it transferred to a glass of water, and have noticed that while the subject is unaffected by the touch of the hand, or even the pricking of a pin, it suffers excruciating pain the moment you touch the surface of the water with the tip of your finger, though the water may have been carried some distance away from the sleeping person. The water becomes highly charged with the sensitiveness of the individual, but loses it in a comparatively short time. On the other hand, a fat or greasy substance will retain the sensitiveness longer ; while, if transferred to a liquid, which is afterwards crystallised, it impregnates the mass for a fortnight, or even longer ; and during the whole of that period the person, when within a reasonable distance, would be conscious if I touched the charged substance, and would suffer pain if I pinched it violently or attempted to stick a pin into it.'

EXTRACT FROM THE 'TIMES' OF DECEMBER 28, 1892.

'There remains, however, one set of recent experiments which, from their novel and startling character, deserve special attention. I refer to the transference of sensibility from a hypnotic subject to inanimate objects. I have been fortunate enough to witness some of these experiments, and will describe what I saw. They were not carried out by Dr. Luys, but by an amateur who attends his clinic.

This gentleman had a roughly-constructed figure, about a foot high, resembling the human form, and made of gutta-percha or some such material, and he experimented with it on a hysterical young woman, one of the hospital patients and an extremely sensitive subject. She was placed in an arm-chair and hypnotised, and he seated himself immediately opposite in close contact with her, their knees touching and her hands placed upon his knees. After some preliminary business of stroking her arms and so forth, he produced the figure and held it up in front of her, presumably to be charged with her magnetism, for these experiments rest on the magnetic theory. Then he placed it out of her sight and pinched it. Sometimes she appeared to feel it and sometimes she did not, but he was all the time in actual contact with her. Then he held it where she could not see it, and this time she obviously suffered acutely whenever he touched the figure and in the place where he touched it, although she did not look at it or seem to observe it. Especially when he touched the sole of the foot it evidently tickled her beyond endurance. Then the figure was placed aside on a table out of sight both of the girl and of the operator, while another gentleman put one hand on the operator's back and the other on the figure. I was in such a position as to see them all, and whenever the second gentleman touched the figure the girl felt it. Then she was told that she was to feel it just the same after being woke up, and an attempt was made to wake her, but she was by this time very profoundly affected, and the attempt was only partially successful. In this state—that is, still som-nambulistic—she stood up and moved from her place. The operator did the same, and being separated from her by some feet he turned his back to her and held the figure in such a position that she could not possibly see it. Then he pinched the back of the figure's neck and the girl felt it at the same moment, but in the wrong place. The place where she did feel it caused her some embarrassment, though harmless enough, as she informed him of the locality in a whisper which I overheard. I can answer for it that she felt something at the moment when he touched the image, and that she could not see it and was not in contact with him, because I was standing almost between them. But she felt it far more acutely when he pinched his own wrist under the same circumstances. That brought the experiments to a conclusion. They occupied at least half an hour, and included a number of interesting details which I have been obliged to omit.

'I shall only offer one comment on this exhibition, which was perfectly genuine. To my mind it in no way proved the transference of sensibility to the image, but it did prove that suggestions and impressions can be conveyed from one person to another by mere contact and even across an intervening space. But that is no new thing in mesmerism. Abundant proof of its occurrence is on record, explain it how you will.'

Other reports of a similar character had appeared in 'La Justice,' 'L'Echo de Paris,' and other French journals.

In subsequent articles I shall describe and illustrate the extraordinary performances here referred to. I have been able by control-experiments on the very subjects here described, and on others who have furnished the basis of many of the lectures and publications by Dr. Luys and Colonel de Rochas, to unmask the deception and credulity which have given rise to these strange proceedings. An extensive and pretentious

G

mass of literature has accumulated around them, and both from the Continent and from this country many persons have been attracted to them, and led to attach to them a scientific value which I shall show to be wholly absent. It is, therefore, a case in which firm and plain words need to be spoken; and I cannot shrink from so doing. It is lamentable that such proceedings should be carried on in the name of science, and that one of the greatest of the Paris hospitals should be made the theatre of such inanities and deceptions. The scientific reputation of a department of a great State institution is seriously affected by these mummeries, and the honour of French medical science is injured before the world when the able journalists of the Continent and Great Britain are hoodwinked by impostors acting under the shelter of the name of a physician who has allowed himself to be their unconscious dupe and enthusiastic patron. Colonel de Rochas is a gentleman of the most undoubted good faith. Neither can any one for a moment doubt the honour and good faith of Dr. Luys, however much we may regret and even blame the persistent credulity he has shown and the inadequacy of the means which he has taken to protect himself and his pupils, his foreign visitors and his right-minded patients from very mischievous deception, and from contact with a certain number of persons, all communication with whom ought for many serious reasons to be shunned. For in connection with some of the subjects of demon-

stration there are underlying questions for the notice
of the police and the correctional tribunals to which I
desire to call the attention of M. Monod and the
Council of the Assistance Publique over which he so
ably and worthily presides.

In order to give an idea of the practices in vogue
in the so-called hypno-therapeutic department of La
Charité Hospital, under the direction of Dr. Luys, and
of the principal performances which are given there, I
will briefly summarise the leading features of some of
those shown to me by M. Luys during several of my
visits to his clinic.   I may mention that both Dr. Lutaud,
who accompanied me on one or two of these visits, and
who had in the first instance communicated with Dr.
Luys on my behalf, and Dr. Sajous, the editor of the
'American Annual of Medical Sciences,' who was also
present on several occasions with me at La Charité, explained to Dr. Luys, at the outset, as I took occasion to
do myself, that I was of a sceptical, as well as of an inquiring turn of mind, with some experience in these
matters, and that it was desirable only to show me
phenomena which he could rely upon as genuine, and
which would bear investigation.

The subjects on whom Dr. Luys demonstrated were
chiefly two patients in the hospital, (1) a man named
Mervel, whom I shall have occasion to mention frequently, and (2) a young woman, Marguerite.   There
were also (3) a girl named Clarice, a former patient,
who arrived at the wards on New Year's day as a

visitor, and who had for a long time previously been a patient and the subject of lectures and demonstrations by Dr. Luys, but who has since, and does now, largely make her living out of her accomplishments, infirmities (and, I must at once add, her tricks), as a trained subject ; (4) a woman, whom I shall speak of as Madame V., who was present at my first visit, having been brought there by Colonel Rochas d'Aiglun, and on whom were displayed all the phenomena known under the mystical and pseudo-scientific names of profound hypnosis, externalisation of sensation, transference of sensibility to inanimate objects, sensitivisation of the atmosphere, &c.; (5) a subject, Jeanne, long an inmate of the hospital and still a subject of demonstration there, who has set up for herself, and is a thriving practitioner as well as a subject in hypnotism. There was some monotony in the repetition of these performances from day to day, so that for the purposes of condensation and classification I shall name them in their generic order, rather than in the precise succession of daily dates in which they occur in my note book.

First, as to the general character of the preliminary phenomena, Dr. Luys professes to base himself on precise experiments demonstrating the principal phenomena of what he calls ' great hypnotism,' as described for the first time in France in masterly fashion by his eminent colleague of the Salpêtrière, Professor Charcot, who would, however, be far from endorsing either the experiments or the conclusions of Dr. Luys. But he

adds to those special researches a series of documents
personal to himself collected in the Charité Hospital,
where he finds a younger, neuropathic population
'nearer the initial period of these maladies, and even
on the borderland of the physiological condition.' I
may say that I found no physiologically sound persons
at the Charité under experiment, but those on whom he
demonstrated were profoundly neuropathic, with the
exception of Madame V. (Colonel Rochas d'Aiglun's
subject), and 'Jeanne,' of whom I shall have much to
say later on, both of whom appeared to be as perfect in
health at the present time as they are in imposture.
Dr. Luys reproaches the Nancy school with having
only studied certain sides of 'minor hypnotism,' and
with having put forward only the phenomena of lucid
somnambulism with concomitant catalepsy and suggestibility, mixed conditions which he considers as inter-
mediate phases and incomplete sketches of the 'greater
hypnotism' imperfectly developed. To these phenomena
of the 'minor hypnotism' he attaches the investigation
of manifestations of 'fascination,' as graphically described
by Brémaud.[1]

Hypnotism Dr. Luys defines as an extra-physiological experimental state of the nervous system, an artificial neurosis which one develops in a predisposed subject, a pseudo-sleep which is imposed and during which

---

[1] Brémaud, 'Sur la Production de l'Hypnotisme chez les Sujets
Sains de Différents Ages,' *Comptes Rendus de la Société de Biologie*,
1863.

the subject under experiment loses the notion of his or her own existence and of the external world. The definition is sufficiently risky and, as will be seen in the sequel, does not apply in its main features to any of the subjects whom he showed me, and who have so often afforded during a series of years the material of his lectures and demonstrations. He recognises, however, very clearly that what he supposes himself to excite experimentally is a true though temporary condition of mental alienation ; the hypnotised individual, he says, having become unconscious of his acts and words and isolated from his surroundings, is reduced to the state of a true transitory lunatic (*aliéné*). He professes to create experimentally many of the disorders of mental pathology in certain stages of hypnotism, and thus to give the factitious but integral representation of some of the disorders of madness. Moreover, he does not conceal from himself the dangers attending these conditions of rapid, almost instantaneous unconsciousness, in which the truly hypnotised subject becomes an inert being, 'a helpless victim to assaults from without.' In the passive state of lethargy or of catalepsy, he says, the subject is absolutely defenceless, exposed to the criminal outrages of those around him or her. A man may be poisoned or mutilated, a woman may be violated and made a mother, or even (as Dr. Luys has known to be the case) infected with syphilis without there existing any trace of the manner in which the outrage was committed, and without the patient preserving the slightest recollection of what has happened. These views and conclusions afford much material for reflection as to possible evils in connection with the general performances at La Charité and with others carried on in private life by persons who had been initiated, apprenticed, and trained there, some of whom still frequent the wards as exhibited subjects, and who carry on hypnotic practices and performances in the outer world with additions, and with all the *éclat* derived from their having been, as they are fond of describing themselves, ' principal subjects ' at La Charité.

Dr. Luys [1] recognises frankly that a great variety of physical methods suffice to produce the condition of artificial sleep—the presentation of a shining object in front of the eyes, the vibrations of a tuning fork, the ticking of a watch, the sound of a horn, a mere word of command, and, when the subject is sufficiently trained, the mere holding of the finger before the eye. To save himself trouble he has had constructed a framework of small mirrors, rotated by a clockwork movement, before which the subjects for experiment are placed, and as they gaze at it they fall into various attidues of slumber, fascination, catalepsy, hysteric hallucination, or whatever else one may please to call it. Fig. 12 (copied from a photograph in a volume of Dr. Luys's lectures) shows the effect of the compound mirror on a

[1] *Leçons Cliniques sur les Principaux Phénomènes de l'Hypnotisme,* par J. Luys. Paris: George Carré, 1890.

number of cataleptic subjects after gazing at it. This mechanical hypnotisation might, it would be supposed, have relieved the physician and those who surround him of some of the superstitions with which his practice is loaded, but it has by no means had that effect.

The first series of phenomena presented to me were illustrative, and supposed to be demonstrative, of the extreme sensitiveness of the hypnotised patient and highly trained subject to magnetic currents however feeble, to residual magnetic impressions, to magnetic effluvia, to the perception of coloured luminous atmospheres radiating from and playing around the poles of a magnet or the anodes of a faradic machine, and to flames and effluvia of like character proceeding from the features, the fingers and the hands of the human subject.

The subject presented to demonstrate these phenomena was the man Mervel, who indeed played a great part in many of the subsequent demonstrations—a sad and unhappy being, extremely pathological in his neurotic aptitudes and infirmities, an undoubted hypnotic and hysteric, but with all the cunning so often super-added to this condition and commonly playing a large part in the clinical picture derived from such performances. I may as well at once give a few outlines of his clinical history, as he told it to me. He came into the wards on November 25, 1891 ; his present illness dated from June 22, when he had fallen from the first floor under an attack of fright when carrying a case weighing 120 lbs.

FIG. 12.—Group of eight persons under the influence of a rotatory mirror apparatus (after Luys).

Three days afterwards he had an attack of lethargy, lasting from eight to twelve hours. He was very well up in the nomenclature of his own case, as indeed are most of these people. He told me he was the victim of heredity, that his father had died of apoplexy, his mother was very nervous, and his sister, when 19 years old, had suffered from attacks of hysterical lethargy. He himself had walked in his sleep while a boy, and was 'born a somnambulist.' Since he had been in the wards he had been treated by prolonged hot baths and lengthened sittings of induced sleep. At one time he said he could not be made to eat, but he had been made to eat 'by suggestion,' and now had a very good appetite. He was still subject to attacks of lethargy and unconsciousness, and had on the previous morning been picked up in the courtyard where he had fallen senseless, and also to fits of somnambulism; he was sleepless, depressed, haggard and altogether a miserable personality. Having put him to sleep, or what looked like hypnotic lethargy, almost instantaneously, by holding two fingers before his eyes, and having rapidly brought him into the lucid stage of somnambulism with the eyelids open, Dr. Luys took into his hand a bar magnet and handed it to the hypnotised Mervel. 'What do you see,' he said, 'from that pole?' Presently Mervel's features, which up to that moment had been expressive only of stupor, became animated and smiling; he caressed the end of the magnet with both hands. 'Ah,' he said with delight, and like a child playing with some beautiful new toy, 'see the blue flames; it's blue, the flames are playing about, it is the colour of the sky—the colour of heaven.' Then the bar was reversed, and the opposite end was shown. 'Ah,' he said, 'that's red.' His features contracted, his brows were knit, his face was expressive of horror and fright. 'Take it away,' he said, 'it's red, red; I don't like it, it hurts me.' Instead of taking it away, however, it was pointed at him. He rose from his seat and moved rapidly away from it backwards, and nearly fell in his retreat to the end of the room. To restore his equanimity the reverse pole was again presented to him. Once more he instantly changed his expression. His features were lighted up with pleasure. 'Ah, c'est bleu;' and he followed the magnet to his seat and fell back into the chair, caressing the magnet as though with extreme delight. These phenomena, Dr. Luys explained to me, were constant, and were related to the attractive and repulsive effects of the north and south poles of the magnet respectively, and to the coloured flames which highly sensitive subjects in the somnambulistic state saw emanating from them.

This proceeding was varied in different forms. Thus on another occasion Dr. Luys took out of his pocket two photographed papers mounted on cardboard and contained in envelopes. One of these, he explained, had been placed in front of a magnet, and the surface of the magnetic pole had been slowly photographed on to it, the other had been simply exposed to the light;

both presented a tolerably uniform and fairly similar blackened surface, but with easily-recognisable differences of coloration. When one of these was presented to the patient he again became ecstatically delighted. 'Ah,' he said, 'it's blue, light blue, the beautiful flames are playing on the surface.' This, it seems, was the magnetic photograph. Then the other was presented to him. He looked at it with a vacuous, indifferent, and uninterested expression. 'Ah,' he said, 'it's dark, it's grey, I don't see anything.' This was the unmagnetised photograph. Again he was shown a photograph of Dr. Luys himself, which he examined with great interest. 'Yes,' he said, 'it is full of lights and colours, there are red flames issuing from the right eye and from the cheek and mouth and ears on one side of the face, and from the other come blue flames, all blue.' 'That,' said Dr. Luys, 'is how he sees me, and, strange to say, the same magnetic flames are seen by him on my photograph. And what is still more remarkable,' added the professor, 'if you give him an illustrated paper he sees blue and red flames radiating from the printed pictures taken from photographs of living individuals, but never from fancy drawings or engravings which have not been photographed from the living subjects in the first instance.'

A further phenomenon and final marvel in this order of ideas was at more than one sitting presented in the same subject. He was thrown into slumber, and a circlet of magnetised iron was placed round his head and forehead. ' In that magnetised head cap,' said Dr. Luys, ' are stored up the thoughts and ideas of a patient who had been the subject of hallucinations of persecution and of black misery. You see that Mervel is now happy and contented enough, but if I now put this magnetised coronet on his head, he will become impregnated with those influences and that order of thought.' This was done, and very quickly his features became haggard, his expression that of melancholy and fear; presently he struggled, with horror and fright depicted in his face, to escape from imaginary persecutors. ' They are following me,' he cried out ; 'I can't get away from them, they are torturing me,' and he endeavoured vainly to escape. Presently the circlet was taken from his forehead, he was told to be calm, and soothed and sent again into profound sleep, then told that he was to awake forgetting all that had happened and to pass a happy day and be very well. He did awake with a dazed look for a short time, and presently said, smilingly, in answer to questions, that he was feeling well, that he did not remember that anything had happened, and that he was going to have a quiet, pleasant day. Dr. Lutaud, who was present with me at this performance in the wards, wickedly observed to Dr. Luys that this newly-found power of storing up habits of mind and thoughts in a magnetic frontal might have some very convenient uses, especially as this set of ideas had already been stored for six months in this particular apparatus apparently not

by any means exhausted by use, and was capable of
application within a period of time of which experience
had not yet prescribed any limits.   It was almost too
much for our gravity when Dr. Luys seriously replied
that no doubt it was so and might be made very useful,
and that he was using such crowns with good therapeutic effects on his patients.   Dr. Lutaud observed
that a husband about to lose a beloved wife might store
up in such a circlet her affectionate thoughts and good
disposition, and might on marrying again infuse these
delightful qualities into the brain of his second wife.
To this, also, Dr. Luys assented.   These were the
leading phenomena presented in connection with the
magnetic susceptibilities and perceptions of the hypnotised subject.   They were repeated on other subjects,
Clarice, and later on, in my own apartments, Jeanne, a
celebrated subject of Luys's lectures, reproduced them
to perfection.   Figs. 13 and 14 are reproductions of two
photographs, which Dr. Luys handed to me as illustrative of the above phenomena of attraction and repulsion
of the negative and the positive poles of the magnet
and of the red and blue flame issuing from them.   He
showed me also a portfolio of drawings for future
publication, in which Mervel in somnambulistic condition had drawn the coloured flames which he saw issuing
from magnets, radiating from the features of Dr. Luys
himself and of various patients, and playing around
the different parts of electro-magnetic apparatus.   At
a later stage Mervel was good enough (always in his

somnambulised state) to favour me with a portrait of the flames which he saw radiating from my eyes and nose and ears. It is an interesting though far from artistic document, which I may reproduce a little later on, when I come to relate the counter-experiments by which I easily demonstrated, in the presence of Dr. Lutaud, Dr. Sajous, M. Cremière, Dr. Olivier, and others, that the whole of these phenomena in all of these patients and subjects were, as might have been expected, frauds, impostures, and simulation, originating, no doubt, in suggestions made to them, lectures given before them, documents communicated to them, and verbal conspiracies hatched in the waiting-room, carried out in the wards, and cleverly worked up by practice to an extraordinary degree of perfection. So wonderfully dramatic were the attitudes and expressions, so graphic, although monotonously similar, were the expressions displayed, so mixed and interwoven were the really hysteric, cataleptic, and somnambulistic conditions presented, heightened and combined by conscious fraud, that it was difficult not to be startled by the extraordinary series of performances shown, and almost impossible at first to divide the basis of reality from the huge superstructure of histrionic fraud and impudent imposture. I may say at once, however, that I succeeded in all of these subjects, and before the same witnesses, and on the same subjects, in reproducing all the phenomena by methods which were quite incompatible with any truthfulness or reality in the acts or in the explanations

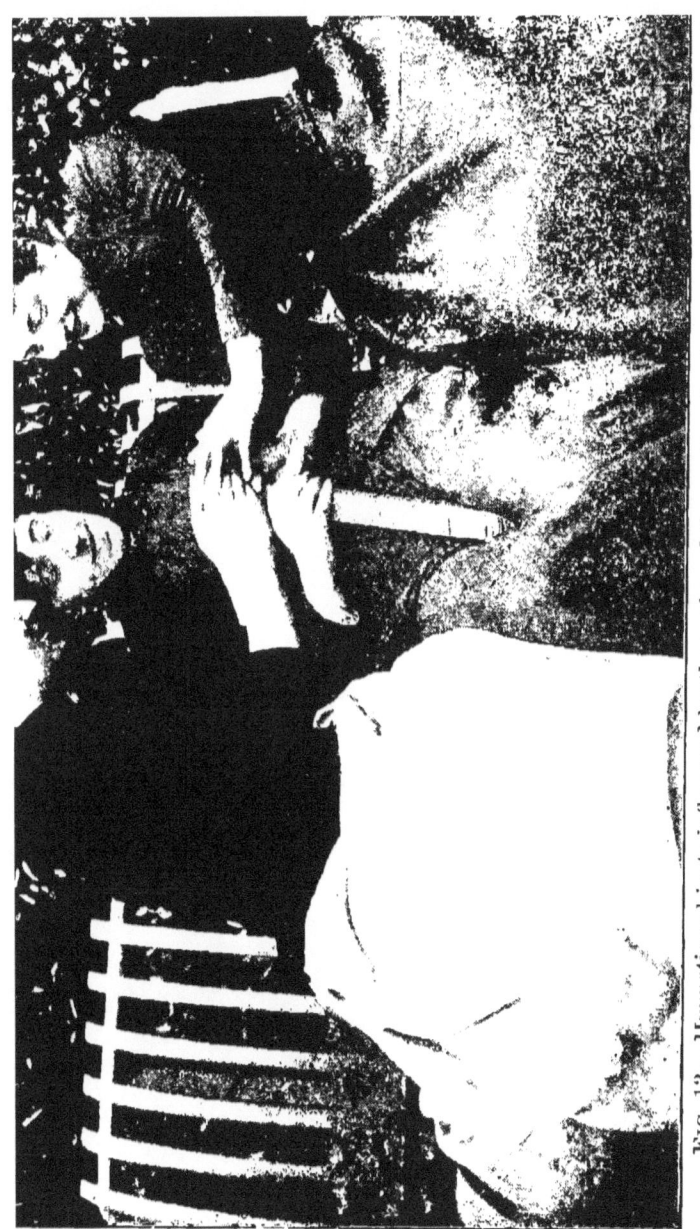

Fig. 13.—Hypnotic subjects influenced by the action of the north pole of a magnet (from a photograph by Dr. Luys).

н 2

given of them; but before proceeding to this part of the
story, I will summarise another series of phenomena
shown to me by Dr. Luys, including some which were
shown to me under his auspices by Colonel Rochas
d'Aiglun on a specially 'susceptible' subject brought to
the wards for the purpose. These were the so-called
emotional and psychical conditions, transfer of thought,
transfer of sensations by contact and at a distance, the
communication by contact from patient to patient of
diseased conditions of body and of mind, the production
of drunkenness in a patient by applying a small sealed
tube containing alcohol to the skin, the transfer of that
drunkenness to another patient by contact of the hands,
the vibrations, as Dr. Luys explained, being probably
transferred from body to body by such contact, the
production of hallucinations and visions by skin contact
with a tube containing medicinal substances, the production of anæsthesia in the patient, and the transfer of
her sensibility to the air surrounding her in different
planes and for given distances, the transfer of her sensibility to a glass of water held in her hand, and similarly
to a wax doll—such sensations, so transferred, being
re-induced in the patient when the glass of water or the
figure was stroked, pinched, pricked, or otherwise tickled
or tortured at a distance from her, and in positions where
it was understood that they could not be seen, and
that she was unaware of what was being done. These
phenomena form another chapter in the strange demonstrations which, to avoid mystification, I may venture

at once by anticipation, however disrespectfully, to describe as fantastic and outrageous, but all of which are
seriously presented as new truths of science to a select
band of students and medical visitors, in this great
Paris hospital. They would hardly be worth serious
notice here but for the sólemn arena in which they are
transacted—a hospital ward in which the 'Times' correspondent stated that fraud was impossible—the solemn
scientific nomenclature under which they are described
and classified, the considerable vogue which has been
given them by the descriptions of eminent journalists,
the extent to which they are already permeating the
higher ranks of society in Paris and attracting ladies of
note from England, and the ramifications with which I
have found them to be connected.

It would occupy too much space to give even a
summarised version of the extraordinary performances
shown in the wards of the Charité as evidences of the
existence of phenomena illustrating the transfer of
sensations by mere contact, the influence of medicines
placed within a sealed tube and brought in contact
with the skin. I shall, therefore, only briefly describe
a few of the things which passed under my eyes and
those of the friends who accompanied me, and will
confine myself especially to those of which I was able
subsequently to seek the verification or refutation by
experiment conducted under somewhat stricter conditions of control than those which Dr. Luys seemed to
think necessary. This physician obtains highly pic-

turesque and truly remarkable results from the mere introduction of substances such as alcohol, pilocarpin, spartein, pepper and valerian in sealed tubes, which he brings into contact with the skin of the neck, placing them inside the collar of the dress.

Operating upon Marguerite, a patient in the wards, on whom I subsequently had the opportunity afforded to me of repeating a controlled experiment, he took from his pocket a tube containing alcohol. Marguerite had already been placed in the required condition of hypnotic sleep, and at the given stage at which these phenomena are supposed to be most readily producible. ' I will now,' he said, ' place this tube of alcohol in contact with her neck, and you will see the result.' I ventured at this point to take M. Luys aside, and suggest to him that, as he had said that he was going to use alcohol, and that as although he believed the patient could not hear him this might be in some minds an open question, he should insert another tube of a different kind from that he had mentioned; but to this suggestion he objected, and insisted on performing his own experiments in his own way. Dr. Luys attaches great importance to the place in which this tube is brought in contact with the skin, and considers that this region of the neck, the seat of great nerve plexuses, freely connecting the cerebro-spinal with the sympathetic system, is an especial point of sensibility. The tube contained about ten drachms of cognac. The effect on Marguerite was very rapid and marked; she began to move her lips and to swallow; the expression of her face changed, and she asked, 'What have you been giving me to drink? I am quite giddy.' At first she had a stupid and troubled look, then she began to get gay. 'I am ashamed of myself,' she said; 'I feel quite tipsy': and after passing through some of the phases of lively inebriety she began to fall from the chair, and was with difficulty prevented from sprawling on the floor. She was uncomfortable, and seemed on the point of vomiting, but this was stopped, and she was calmed.

Clarice, another hypnotic, a former patient and what is termed a highly-trained subject, who is now pursuing a career outside of the hospital, and who had looked in on a visit, was hypnotised, and placed in a chair alongside of Marguerite. Her hand and that of Marguerite were clasped together. 'Now,' said Dr. Luys, 'we will see if the vibrations characteristic of this nervous condition will be transferred by contact from one to the other.' Very shortly Clarice went through the same stages; she, too, presently became giddy, facially disturbed, disordered in gesture. She passed through the stages of drunken gaiety and then of profound inebriety with muscular resolution. The performance was completed by waiting a few minutes in order that the effect which, as Dr. Luys observed, had been produced by the cognac on the nervous system of the subject, might be dissipated.

As another order of phenomena was to be demon-

strated that day according to the programme, no more
tubes were then introduced, but on another visit we
witnessed a similar and even yet more dramatic incident of the same kind. This was the influence upon
the organism of valerian in a sealed tube.   The
subject on whom this phenomenon was intended to
be exhibited was Jeanne, of whom I have already
spoken, who is a favourite subject for Dr. Luys's demonstrations, and of whose sincerity and remarkable
endowments he speaks in various parts of his lectures
with much enthusiasm. For reasons, however, of a
very prosaic order, which Jeanne subsequently explained
to me, she did not think it worth while to appear at
the thinly attended clinic of the holiday season, the
period of my visit.   The ever-faithful Mervel was therefore utilised for the valerian performance, although, as
Dr. Luys explained, he was not sure it would succeed.
Mervel's accomplishments, however, were undervalued.
He did succeed, and the event came off to perfection.
When the valerian tube was placed in contact with his
sterno-mastoid, his face expressed first great amazement,
then total change of expression, with singular muscular
contortions ; presently he began to twist about strangely
in his chair, clawing the air.   As I was not prepared
for the sequel, I spoke to him and asked him what was
the matter.   In many previous experiments he had
answered quite intelligently the questions which I had
put to him in his hypnotic state, which a little surprised
me, for I was not supposed to be *en rapport* with him,

and it is often stated that hypnotised patients can only answer questions put by the actual operator. This, however, did not appear to be the case with any of the subjects at the Charité, and, in fact, I have often observed that this is a matter of training, and that in point of fact such patients can or cannot answer by-standers, according as they think they may or can. In this case, however, Mervel was mute. ' He cannot answer you,' explained Dr. Luys. ' He is being trans-formed into a cat, and cats cannot speak ; and therefore he cannot speak.'   Presently the unhappy being threw himself on to the floor, sprawling on all fours, and began clawing, scratching the boards, making little leaps and springs of an awkwardly feline character, then spitting like a tom cat, and mewing. He followed us across the room with the simulated actions of a highly-excited human cat, scratching at our clothes, mewing, and becoming very much excited, with a livid and congested face. For pity's sake I begged that the performance might be ended, and he was put back in his chair, quieted, and presently brought to himself. He pro-fessed to have no recollection of anything that had happened. These were the only two experiments of the kind which I saw in Dr. Luys's wards, but I will quote from one of his lectures his own account of simi-lar experiments on other subjects, illustrated by drawings from his own photographs :—

' Here is, in fact, a second tube containing 10 grammes of distilled water. I place the tube in the

same place as before, and you will see the specific
character of the phenomena which are about to be displayed. In this case the subject does not quite reach
the stage of somnambulism, he does not speak, the
phenomena start from the great apparatus of respiration; it is the laryngeal nerves that are put in action.
You hear a noise of whistling inspiration, then a true
stridor from development of spasm of the glottis.   At
the same time the thyroid region swells, the face becomes congested, and the masseter muscles are in a
condition of trismus.   It is impossible to open the
mouth ; it is a real stage of artificial hydrophobia which
is thus induced by the action of water; and if the
process is allowed to go on, you see that this tetanic
state of the muscles of the jaws spreads to the back and
the limbs, and we see pass rapidly before us a true
generalised tetanus.   In order to bring all this series
of symptoms to an end—since if they were prolonged
by guilty hands they might evidently bring about grave
complications in connection with the thoracic viscera—
I quickly remove the tube, and you see that on this
occasion as on the former, *sublatâ causâ tollitur effectus*.
The respiratory movements become regular, relaxation
of the muscles insensibly takes place, and Gabrielle
returns to a stage of normal lethargy.

'After having at the end of some minutes ascertained that the subject has got rid (by the return of
neuro-muscular contractility) of the last traces of shock
which she has previously undergone, I present to her

this tube containing a 1 in 10 solution of sulphate of spartein. The reaction will here be as significant as possible, and altogether different from those effects you have hitherto seen. Take note of them as they pass, because I am unable to prolong these experiments, so great, in my opinion, is the risk of causing unforeseen accidents in connection with the thoracic viscera. You see that I place the tube in the same place, and I consequently provoke a reaction by means of the same underlying nervous plexuses. It is evident that the laryngeal, pneumogastric, and sympathetic nerves are sharply stimulated. See, indeed, what occurs with increasing rapidity. The subject at first exhibits some contractures of the face ; then instantaneously the respiratory movements become accelerated and are repeated in an anxious manner ; then they stop, and with astonishment you behold that they cease completely. At the same time note the swelling of the thyroid body, how the face becomes turgid and purple, and how the beatings of the arteries show themselves in the neck with excessive fulness ; the sight of this enormous distension of the capillary system in the face makes one think of a possible rupture of the arterial walls, which, however little brittle they may be, might set up instantaneous hæmorrhages to a more or less serious extent. I do not insist, gentlemen, on this experiment, which I never repeat without a certain dread. You see the powerful action which bodies at a distance produce on a subject in a state of hypnotism. These are new conditions of receptivity thus created in the human organism, and I believe it to be my duty from the medico-legal point of view to give you a sample of these complex phenomena which open up new vistas in the domain of crime. I will in your presence awaken Gabrielle in the usual way, and you will not be surprised if you see, on her awakening, how unconscious she is of all the disturbances she has undergone in her inner being, and at the same time that she retains no recollection of the previous experiments.

'I now present, as a second subject, Esther, who has already appeared before you. I put her to sleep in the usual way, and as soon as she is in a state of lethargy I place at the side of her neck this same tube filled with cognac. Wait some seconds and see what is about to take place. At first some grimaces occur, followed by movements of the tongue and lips, as when one tastes a liquid ; next, passing like Gabrielle into the stage of somnambulism, she utters broken sentences: " I am thirsty--I want a drink—give me a drink." The speech is that of a drunken person ; the voice is thick and the tongue sluggish. She says : " I am drunk without drinking." She tries to get up from the arm-chair and falls back heavily, doubled up on herself. I remove the tube and you then see the same symptoms which you have before seen take place occur in reverse order—namely, the movements of tasting and the grimaces. Esther ends by falling back into lethargy. I wait some minutes for the shock which has gone through her nervous system to disappear, and after having recognised, by means of the return of normal muscular hyperexcitability in the forearms, that this effect is exhausted, I apply to the neck the tube previously used, but now containing water. Almost immediately you see strange phenomena occur, which develop in the stage of catalepsy without somnambulism. Instantaneously Esther's face assumes an expression of terror, her eyes are widely open, haggard, and fixed; the features of the countenance are motionless, the masseters rigid, which makes it impossible to open the mouth. In a few cases I have even seen saliva flow from the mouth like froth, at the same time the muscles of the tongue become rigid, and a generalised tetanic condition develops. If you examine these symptoms as a whole, are you not led to see in the general expression of the subject the experimental symptomatology of hydrophobia? And the tube which provokes all these disturbances only contains 10 grammes of water. I do not insist on this, and I content myself for the moment with calling your attention to this effect—namely, that the reaction which has just taken place in Esther before you is entirely different from that produced by the previous tube containing cognac. I take away the tube, and you see that the ascending march of the phenomena observed is interrupted, and that little by little the subject, deprived of the incitatory stimuli supplied by the external agent, instantaneously falls back into the stage of lethargy from which she had been roused by

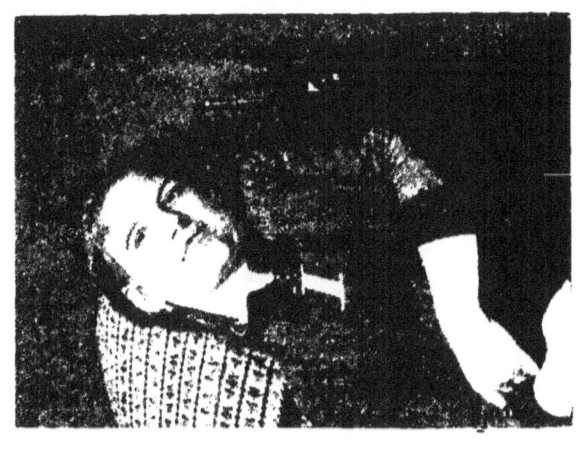

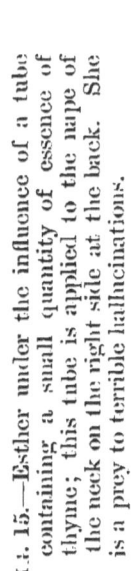

Fig. 15.—Esther under the influence of a tube containing a small quantity of essence of thyme; this tube is applied to the nape of the neck on the right side at the back. She is a prey to terrible hallucinations.

Fig. 16.—Esther under the influence of hydrochlorate of morphine. The tube has been placed in front of the left eye, and the face expresses very clearly a state of beatitude.

FIG. 17.—Esther is influenced by a tube containing sulphate of strychnine. The tube is presented at the right side. She seems to be listening to something droll, which makes her laugh.

FIG. 18.—The same tube has been placed in front of the right eye of the same subject. Inverse phenomena. The face expresses profound terror.

I

means of it.   I wait a few minutes before applying the
third tube, in order that the muscular excitability may
return.   This, I repeat, is of the greatest importance in
order to avoid the risk of the successive reactions of
the nervous system being influenced or even entirely
modified one by the other.

'I now place the third tube, containing the spartein
solution, close to the neck.   Hardly has it been placed
there before reaction begins, as you see.   The nerves
of the neck, in a condition of hyperexcitability, instantaneously transmit to the centres the new incitations
which act upon them.   The respiratory movements are
quickened, as you may see; respiration becomes em-
barrassed; you even hear stridor now and then; at the
same time redness and cyanosis of the face and a characteristic turgescence of the eyes announce to you that a
profound disturbance has taken place in the circulatory
apparatus.   The veins of the neck are swollen, there is
an expression of terror in the face, the movements of
respiration stop, and, if I keep the tube in position any
longer, you will see the breathing cease altogether.   In
presence of phenomena so characteristic, of disturbances so great, re-echoing through all the main parts of
the human machine, is it possible, I ask you, gentlemen,
to believe that these things are simulated, as a certain
number of people who have never made the smallest
experiment themselves are so ready to repeat?   Whatever desire hysterical subjects may have to make themselves interesting (a desire in which I myself have only

a very limited belief), it is unquestionable that this desire can in no sort of way lead them thus madly to jeopardise their existence.

'The interests of science make it necessary that these delicate experiments should be studied and followed up. I never practise them without the greatest precautions, taking care to employ only minimum doses of active medicinal substances, and to produce in the subjects only fugitive effects which are not dangerous for them. Nevertheless, from the medico-legal point of view, penetrate yourselves thoroughly with the consequences which may follow from all that you have just seen. Who, in fact, shall tell us that these symptoms of impending asphyxia and of obstruction of the great vessels, if produced by criminal hands, might not cause pulmonary congestion with hæmoptysis, ruptures of the vessels or of an aneurism, perhaps stoppage of the heart, and then murder having been committed under such circumstances, how shall the cause of death be recognised, and how shall the guilty person be discovered? I have now taken away the tube containing spartein, and you see that a general reaction takes place. Esther begins to breathe regularly, the circulatory apparatus recovers its equilibrium, quiet is insensibly re-established, and we arrive, as you see, at the stage of lethargy. I now awaken the subject in the usual way; Esther, passing successively through the stages of catalepsy and somnambulism, reaches the stage of waking, and opens her eyes naturally. She has, as you see, no recollection of what has passed, but, if her memory is dumb, yet a vague sense of fatigue of muscular sensibility persists, and after these disturbing experiments she usually feels out of sorts and slightly depressed during the day.'

I will now pass to the description of the series of experiments which I carried out on the five subjects whom I named at the outset as being those who were presented to me by Dr. Luys and Colonel de Rochas respectively. Meantime I observe that Dr. Luys has stated in the 'Times' of January 31 (the date on which I am writing the present chapter of my experiences) that I was 'unlucky enough to apply to patients to whom he had long ceased to have recourse, being unable to depend on their veracity.'

The patients to whom I had recourse were Marguerite ——, who was the patient actually in the wards of the Charité, and on whom Dr. Luys carried out, to use his own words, in my presence and that of Dr. Lutaud, Dr. Sajous, and M. Cremière, 'experiments relative to the psychical action, either attractive or repulsive, of the different poles of a magnetic bar on hypnotised patients.' 'I also showed him,' Dr. Luys continues, 'that glass tubes, containing either brandy or tincture of valerian, applied to the same patients, could determine on them effects peculiar to those substances.' In addition to this, Dr. Luys observes that he ' gave a few simple experiments and demonstrations, showing Mr. Hart, for instance, that when persons are hypnotised, their usual faculties are raised to an extra-physiological pitch, and that the patients see things that we cannot in our normal state distinguish; thus they behold the waves which are developed from a polarised bar, or from a magnetic needle, with their different colouring.' These experiments also were conducted by Dr. Luys at different sittings upon Marguerite and upon Mervel, as I have already described. Dr. Luys considers that the statement which I have published of the results of my control experiments incriminate his honour as a man of science. I have, so far as I know, carefully avoided any comments which could be construed in that sense, although I have thought myself more than justified in intimating that he has pushed negligence in a so-called scientific investigation, put forward by him in great detail and with great solemnity for many years, to the utmost verge of blamable want of carefulness. This I shall have no difficulty in proving up to the hilt, and I shall adduce evidence which is incontrovertible, and rests not only on my own observation but on that of highly competent and independent observers who were present at my experiments, and who have signed the notes of the sittings.

As to the statement which Dr. Luys now makes—that these subjects were persons to whom he had long ceased to have recourse, being unable to depend upon their veracity—I do not know how to characterise it in any terms which in a matter of this sort I should be

willing to employ.   In the first place I must point out
that if Jeanne, Marguerite, Mervel, and Clarice, the four
persons whom he brought under my notice and on whom
I operated, have long been known to Dr. Luys as persons who were untruthful and guilty of gross impostures ; then he charges himself with going solemnly in
the wards through a series of performances which he
presented to me, to Drs. Lutaud and Sajous, and
to M. Cremière as reliable evidences of the phenomena
he undertook to demonstrate on them.   It was with
Marguerite, with Mervel and with Clarice that he
went through the performances of which he speaks and
that I have already described.   It was on Marguerite
and Clarice that he demonstrated, as he states in his
letter, the drunkenness supposed to result from placing
a tube containing alcohol in contact with the skin, and
the transfer by contact from Marguerite to Clarice of
that drunkenness.   It was on Marguerite that in his
presence Colonel de Rochas, whom he describes as his
fellow-labourer and friend, demonstrated what Dr. Luys
also describes as the Colonel's real and extraordinary discoveries of the externalisation of sensation, of the transfer
of sensation to the air and to glasses of water.   It was
on Mervel that Dr. Luys demonstrated the extraordinary performance of the transformation of a man into
a cat by the contact of a small tube containing valerian.
It was on Mervel that he also showed the extra-physiological acuteness of vision, which enabled this man to
behold the waves developed from a polarised bar or

from a magnetic needle, with their different colouring. It was on these subjects, and no others, except Madame Vix and Jeanne, that I operated ; and it was with these subjects that I ascertained and proved to the satisfaction of those who saw the experiments that the whole performance was a gross imposture.　If Dr. Luys knew, as he now says that he knew, that the subjects were impostors, that knowledge, or even the present affirmation of it, would place him in a position which I would be most unwilling to believe—nay, which I do not for a moment believe—him to occupy.　I cannot suppose, and will not allow myself to admit, that he was presenting to us as subjects for scientific demonstration in his wards persons whom he had long known to be false and untrustworthy.　I prefer to think that his letter was written under a sense of·irritation, and that the statement to which I refer is one made by him without due reflection and which he will not be willing ultimately to maintain.　For Madame Vix he is not directly responsible ; though she was the subject brought by Colonel de Rochas to his wards and presented to me there.　She was as great an impostor as the others, and Dr. Luys's affirmation of the reality of the phenomena which she presented is nothing worse than a merely reckless and irresponsible endorsement of the veracity of an utterly unreliable woman who subsequently showed herself in the opinion of myself and my friends to be a deliberate falsifier of facts.

There is one other point worthy of Dr. Luys's serious consideration in this matter. If he is willing to admit that Jeanne and Clarice are persons utterly unworthy of belief, as I have proved them to be, and as he now alleges that he has long known them to be, then I must ask him, and I do ask him very directly and very seriously, what reliance can be placed on the whole volume of clinical lectures from which I have been quoting? Jeanne is the woman whose photograph he gave me on the last day of my visit to his clinic, represented as sitting with two others, presenting the most vivid image of delight and attraction towards the blue flames and influenced by the action of the north pole of the magnet, and repelled and horrified under the influence of the south pole. His book is full of Jeanne, and he is warm in his eulogies of her exquisite sensibility for hypnotic phenomena, and vouches for her sincerity. He speaks of her sometimes as Jeanne and sometimes as Mademoiselle V., a professor of foreign languages.

I ask Dr. Luys, then, to explain why, if he knew Jeanne and Clarice to be impostors, he presented them, together with Marguerite and Mervel, as witnesses of the truth only some weeks ago? How it is that he has not withdrawn those parts of his lectures which he bases on their performances; and I ask him further to state explicitly who it is among the subjects of my experiments, chosen from his own subjects as being the only persons produced by him, whom he now

denounces as having long been known to him as untrustworthy ?

I did not raise the question of good faith in respect
of Dr. Luys; on the contrary, I expressly declared my
belief in his good faith, alleging my conviction that,
as these women themselves openly said to me in the
presence of M. Cremière and others, Dr. Luys was
their dupe. The words of Jeanne were : '*Nous le
flouons, tous.*' I gave him credit, and still give him
credit, for perfect good faith, although I charge him
with incredible looseness in his method of experiment,
and with incredible extravagance and error in the
deductions which he has allowed himself to make from
the false phenomena to which his mode of experimenta-
tion inevitably leads. He has now raised the question of his own good faith by alleging that he knew
and has long known these subjects to be destitute of
veracity, and he must settle that question with himself
rather than with me. On that subject I am ready to
accept whatever declaration Dr. Luys, after full recon-
sideration of his position, may desire to make. I am
satisfied that in such a matter he will be incapable of
doing anything which is not fully worthy of his distinguished position as a member of the Academy of
Medicine and a physician of one of the great French
hospitals. I am satisfied, too, and shall now produce
the evidence, that neither Jeanne, nor Mervel, nor
Clarice, nor Marguerite is worthy of the slightest
credence in anything which they assert they saw or felt

or did in respect to any of these performances. But when did Dr. Luys become convinced of this, and, being convinced of it, when and to whom did he first announce it, or first give the warnings due to himself as having acted before the world and to me and those who were with me so late as January 5, as the sponsor of their sincerity?

I turn now to my notes of the results of some of the tests applied by me to Dr. Luys's subjects. I repeated on Marguerite, in the presence of two witnesses, most of the experiments which had been performed on her by Colonel de Rochas in the wards of Dr. Luys and in his presence. Dr. Luys had reproduced with her the phenomena of the influence of medicines at a distance, and with her and Clarice jointly the transmission of drunkenness by contact of one patient with the other. On January 6 Marguerite came to my rooms in charge of a medical friend. We began by hypnotising her after the classic method of M. de Rochas and Dr. Luys, putting her through the successive stages already described. I had prepared an electro-magnet of considerable power, from which the current could be turned on or off with great rapidity by touching a button or by lifting the plates from the bath, or of course by detaching one or other of the wires. I had also a bar of iron resembling the magnetised bar which M. Luys had used, but which was not magnetic, a demagnetised magnet, and a set of needles variously and inversely magnetised. I had also two exactly similar wax dolls brought from a toy shop, and two exactly similar glasses of water. We began the proceedings by the *prise du regard*, which was perfectly performed; we then used the magnets. I signalled to the assistant, and told him to put on the current, whereupon he turned it off. Accustomed, however, to believe that a magnet must be a magnet, Marguerite began to handle it. The note taken by Dr. Sajous runs thus: ' She found the north pole, notwithstanding there was no current, very pretty; she was as it were fascinated by it; she caressed the blue flames, and showed every sign of delight. Then came the phenomena of attraction. She followed the magnet with delight across the room, as though fascinated by it; the bar was turned so as to present the other end, or what would be called, in the language of La Charité, the south pole, then she fell into the attitude of repulsion and horror, with clenched fists, and as it approached her she fell backward into the arms of M. Cremière, and was carried, still showing all the signs of terror and repulsion, back to her chair. The bar was again turned until what should have been the north pole was presented to her, she resumed the same attitudes of attraction, and tears bedewed her cheeks. " Ah," she said, " it is blue, the flames mount," and she rose from her seat, following the magnet round the room. Again the pole bar was reversed, and once more she exclaimed that she saw " all red, all red." ' Similar but false phenomena were obtained in succession with all the different forms of magnet and non-

FIG. 19.—A ' Witness ' Doll used in
Control Experiments.

FIG. 20.—A ' Witness ' Doll used in
Control Experiments.

magnet; Marguerite was never once right, but throughout her acting was perfect; she was utterly unable at
any time really to distinguish between a plain bar of
iron, demagnetised magnet, or a horse-shoe magnet
carrying a full current and one from which the current
was wholly cut off. In the latter part of this sitting
Dr. Olivier entered the room and witnessed the second
series of magnetic experiments as well as the experiments of externalisation. We took one of the dolls.
We restored Marguerite to the perfectly hypnotised condition, and when she was profoundly plunged in the
state which is described as profound hypnosis, I placed
a doll in her hand, which she held long enough to sen-
sitise it. I then, taking the doll from her, rapidly
disposed of it behind some books, and proceeded to
operate on another doll which she had not touched and
which I had just taken out of the box in which it came
from the toy-shop. The preceding illustrations show the
witness dolls with which I operated (figs. 19 and 20).
Holding her hand I placed her in contact with Dr.
Sajous, that he might also be, to use the jargon of the
school, *en rapport* with her, and I continued to hold her
hand. If now I touched the hair of the doll, which she
was supposed not to see, she exclaimed, according to
my notes, ' On touche les cheveux,' ' On les tire '—
' They are touching my hair—they are pulling it '—and
as she complained it hurt her, we had to leave off
pulling the doll's hair. Taking the doll to a little
distance, I pinched it; she showed every sign of pain,

and cried out 'I don't like to be hurt—je ne veux pas qu'on me fasse de mal.' I tickled the cheek of the figure, she began to smile pleasantly (I am still quoting from the notes). I put away the witness dolls, and we then proceeded to the effects of medicine tubes applied to the skin. I took a tube which was supposed to contain alcohol, but which did contain cherry laurel water. She immediately began, to use the words of M. Sajous's note, to smile agreeably and then to laugh; she became gay: 'It makes me laugh,' she said, and then, 'I'm not tipsy, I want to sing,'—and so on through the whole performance of a not ungraceful *griserie* which we stopped at that stage, for I was loth to have the degrading performance of drunkenness carried to the extreme I had seen her go through at the Charité. I now applied a tube of alcohol, asking the assistant, however, to give me valerian, which no doubt this profoundly hypnotised subject perfectly well heard, for she immediately went through the whole cat performance I have already described as having been performed for my delectation by Mervel under the hands of Dr. Luys on the previous day. She spat, she scratched, she mewed, she leapt about on all-fours, and she was as thoroughly cat-like as was Mervel on the previous and Jeanne on the subsequent day. It would be tedious to go through the whole of the notes of the numerous sittings which I had with these five subjects, but I may say at once that we had the cat performance six times, twice with Jeanne, twice with

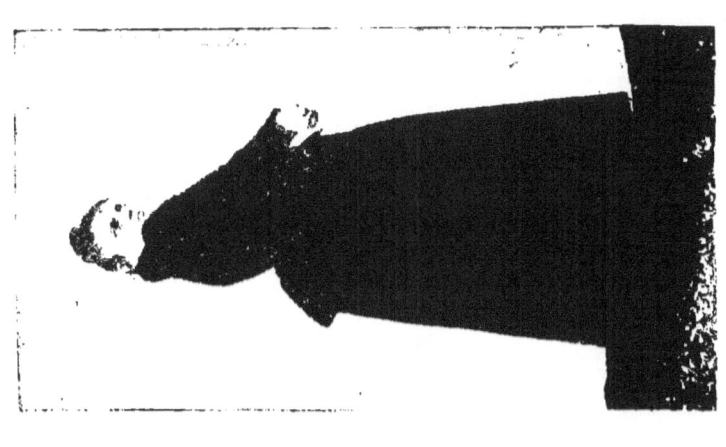

FIG. 22.—Clarice 'hypnotised' and repelled by a blue glass ball.

FIG. 21.—Clarice 'hypnotised' and attracted by a yellow glass ball.

K

Vix, once with Clarice, and once with Mervel.   In no case by any accident was valerian used, but either sugar, alcohol, diabetic sugar, cherry laurel water or distilled water; nevertheless the performance never failed when the subjects had reason to think it was expected of them.

Space will not permit me to reproduce the protocols of the various sittings in Paris, at which I tested the unreality of the hypnotic phenomena presented to me at the Charité.   I retain for reference and for verification the original documents, signed by the various witnesses who were present, and who minutely watched all my counter-experiments.   I had very numerous sittings and carried out in the methods above described numerous and complete counter-tests, selecting always and only the patients who had been presented to me by Dr. Luys and Colonel de Rochas, and the subjects who had been operated on.   Never by any accident did any one of these subjects show any power of discerning the effects of magnetised from non-magnetised iron; the pretension of Dr. Luys that they could distinguish between magnetic photographs so-called and non-magnetic were in every case ascertained to be unfounded; the communication of sensations or thought by contact never took place in any case unless the subjects knew precisely what was the nature of the comedy to be played, and then they played it more or less well.   The cat performance and the drunken scenes came off six times when the sub-

ject supposed that the tubes contained alcohol, but
when they really contained divers substances, none of
which were alcoholic ; the scenes produced were acted
in the same way under the influence of an empty tube, of
a tube of alcohol, and of a tube of valerian.   In order
that there may be no doubt of the accuracy of these
statements, I reproduce the letters of three eye-witnesses.

Dr. de Cyon, the well-known physiologist, writes,
under date January 28, 1893 :—

I can testify that the experiments at which I was
present took place exactly as you have described them.
The methods which you employed to demonstrate the
trickery on the part of the subjects— notably the changing
of the dolls and the substitution of the glass of water and
of the magnet—were so simple that one finds a difficulty in
believing that the physicians who have made themselves
the apostles of this new superstition are acting in good
faith.   I have myself made numerous experiments on Dr.
Luys's subjects and of those of many other physicians ;
and I have always succeeded with the greatest facility
in unmasking their frauds, which really can only deceive
those who wish to be deceived.   Either dupes or accomplices—there is no other alternative term for the adepts of
the doctrines now tending to discredit medicine and to
throw it back many centuries.   I am entirely in agreement with what you have said as to the morality of the
subjects who lend themselves to these grotesque experiments.   This branch of the subject much more concerns
the *police des mœurs* than it does clinical medicine.

Dr. Louis Olivier, D.Sc., Editor of the 'Revue

Générale des Sciences pures et appliquées,' writes, January 19, 1893 :—

I am quite ready to relate what I saw at the sittings which took place in your room in the Hôtel Continental. There was no accord between the phenomena manifested by the hypnotised subjects and the production of the current of magnetisation, &c. You repeated the experiments of Dr. Luys and those of M. de Rochas, avoiding all suggestion, either involuntary or unconscious, which might vitiate the results. You took care to hide from the subjects the nature of the drugs tested, to which M. Luys attributes an action at a distance, and the moment of the closure or opening of the current of your electro-magnet. Under these conditions there was no longer any relation between the nature of the medicinal agent and the symptoms manifested ; when the circuit was opened without their knowledge, the subjects said they experienced the varied sensations which they ordinarily attribute to the passage of the current. They were unable to distinguish the open from the closed state of the current. You repeated M. de Rochas's experiment of *envoûtement*, employing without the knowledge of the hypnotised woman two dolls, one of which remained carefully separated from her. She uttered shrieks when I pulled the hair of the doll which she had not touched, &c. These facts appear to me decisive in regard to the settlement of a question which I ought to say has been decided by the vast majority of the French scientific public in a sense absolutely opposed to the results proclaimed by MM. Luys and de Rochas. It is well that it should be known in England that the opinions of these two experimenters find no support in the French scientific world.

Dr. Lutaud, the Editor of the ' Journal de Médecine de Paris,' writes :—

I have read with most lively interest in the ' British Medical Journal' your notes on the New Mesmerism, and I hasten to state that you have reproduced very faithfully the opinion of all those who were present at the Paris experiments, and that your judgment, although severe, is absolutely just.

I pass now to the consideration of the underlying substratum of fact on which this huge structure of imposture and credulity is built. As I have already sufficiently indicated, the artificially induced sleep known by the old-fashioned Latin name somnambulism, or subsequently as mesmerism, and rebaptized in Greek, hypnotism, as though it were a new thing, is a subjective phenomenon of great interest, and of some complexity. It is, perhaps, not altogether unworthy of the attention which has been bestowed on it by French and German physicians. On the other hand— and here I only express a purely personal opinion, which must be taken for just what it is thought to be worth—I at least have come to the conclusion, after carefully watching the course of events at the Salpêtrière and Bicêtre, and studying the enormously voluminous literature which owes its origin to the school of Nancy, to the Paris school, and to Belgian and Austrian writers, that the importance of these studies has been vastly exaggerated. I am disposed to think that it is more the picturesque eccentricity of the phenomena and the striking *mise en scène* to which human automatism lends itself and which has attracted so much attention, than the real medical or physiological importance of the subject. Hypnotism, even as practised at the Salpêtrière, has, so far as I can see, taught us little, if anything, of the functions of the brain or of the organs of the mind that we did not know before. I find little in the writings of Charcot, of Bernheim, or of Janet but an excessively detailed development of facts and principles, already soundly, clearly and usefully laid down by Carpenter and Braid. With a lucidity, clinical power, and picturesqueness beyond praise, M. Charcot has described, depicted and exemplified a most striking series of hysterical phenomena. He has shown that nearly, if not quite all hypnotics, are neurotic persons to whom the general classification of hysterics or neurasthenics may fairly be applied.

Of the intrinsic correctness of his classification of the stages of hysteria in its larger forms, I am sceptical ; nor do I think it a permanent nosological classification which will endure in medicine. These various stages, so regularly produced in classical order, appear to be performances originating partly in the auto-suggestion of an originally morbid patient, and then perpetuated by imitation, suggestion, ward training, and by habit in some. I am so persuaded that they are artificial, that I even venture to predict they will cease to exist when the succession, so to speak, of M. Charcot's trained patients is broken, and when the habit of performance in the wards and theatre of the Salpêtrière is given up, as I am inclined to think it will be before long. Such patients and such stages of the greater hysteria are not found elsewhere, unless the patients are led up to them by training or by imitative instincts; they are non-natural, they have no real existence in medicine and will take no enduring place, so far as one can judge, in the history of medicine. It was natural enough that one extravagance should lead to another, and the follies of La Charité can but be regarded as the offspring—illegitimate, perhaps, and repudiated—of certain extravagances into which even men so able, so lucid and so thoughtful as the School of the Salpêtrière have allowed themselves to be led. Already there are, happily, signs of a reaction within the School of the Salpêtrière itself. I believe that journalists and the public are now excluded from these performances; the *grande hystérie*, with all its stages, is much more rarely seen, and there is reason to hope that it will die out now that the first excitement of this scenic display has weakened and the performance is felt to be monotonous and wearisome. Thought transference is not now spoken of at La Salpêtrière and the proceedings at La Charité are there ignored with an intentionally contemptuous silence.

What remains, then, of practical value and of medical utility as the results of these lengthened studies? What are their mischiefs? Are these adequately balanced against their benefits? First as to their mischiefs. I will again let Dr. Luys speak, for although he is the most enthusiastic apostle of the presumed benefits, he is perfectly outspoken as to the resultant injuries.

'From the social point of view these new states of instantaneous loss of consciousness into which hypnotic or merely fascinated subjects may be made to pass deserve to be considered with lively interest. As I shall have to explain to you later, the individual in these novel conditions no longer belongs to himself; he is surrendered, an inert being, to the enterprise of those who surround him. At one moment in the passive stage in this condition of lethargy or of catalepsy, he is absolutely defenceless, and exposed to any criminal attempt on the part of those who surround him. He can be poisoned and mutilated. Where a woman is concerned she may be violated and even infected with syphilis, of which I have recently observed a painful example in my practice. She may become a mother without any trace existing of a criminal assault, and without the patient having the smallest recollection of what has passed after she has awakened. Sometimes, in the active condition, the state of lucid somnambulism, and even in the condition of simple fascination, the subject may be exposed to the influence of suggestions of the most varied kind on the part of the person directing his actions. He may be induced to become a homicide, an incendiary, or suicide, and all these impulses deposited in his brain during sleep become forces silently stored up, which will burst forth at a given moment with the precision, accuracy of performance and automatic impetuosity of acts performed by the really insane.

'Gentlemen, bear this well in mind; all these acts, all these phenomena unconsciously accomplished, are no mere vague apprehensions and vain suppositions; they are real facts which you may meet with every day of ordinary life. They are prone to develop, and to appear around you and before you in the most inexplicable manner.'[1]

In many places Dr. Luys cautions his pupils against the dangers that may arise if hypnotic patients fall into the hands of unscrupulous persons. The hypnotised patient he describes as malleable, flexible and obedient in a completely passive fashion. 'You can,' he says, page 193, *et seq.*, 'not only oblige this defence-less being incapable of resistance to make you a manual gift, but to sign a promise, a bill of exchange, to write a holograph will in your favour, and to hand it you without his ever knowing what it contains or even that it exists. He will accomplish the most minute legal formalities calmly and serenely, so that the most experienced officers of the law would be deceived. Here is Esther. She will write and sign before you a deed of gift in my favour good for a thousand francs. Her

---

[1] *Leçons cliniques sur les principaux Phénomènes de l'Hypnotisme dans leurs Rapports avec la Pathologie Mentale.* Par J. Luys. Paris: Georges Carré, éditeur, 58 Rue St. André-des-Arts, 1890.

FIG. 23.—Esther in the normal state.

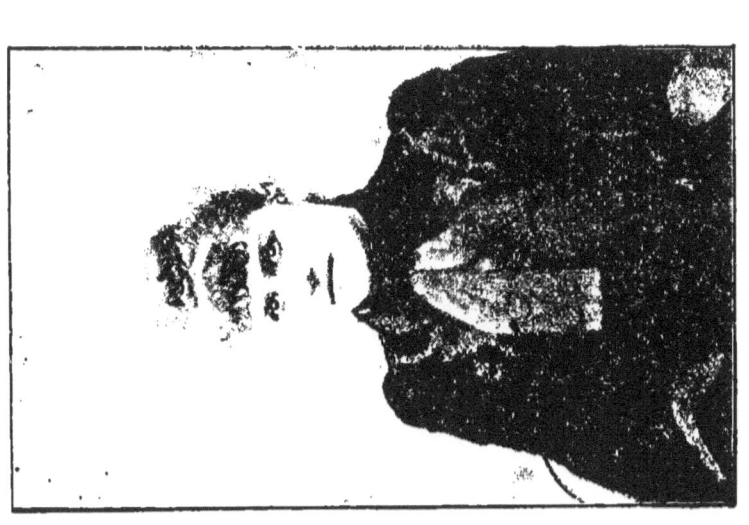

FIG. 24.—Esther suddenly and profoundly alarmed by the luminous radiation of a bottle cork.

writing is as good in her hypnotised as in her wakeful
state, perhaps firmer and less hesitating. You could
make her swallow, as you see, a bread pill, thinking it
to be a peppermint lozenge; if it were a capsule containing morphine, and she was to be awakened as the
victim of poisoning, she would know nothing of the
origin of her symptoms. If I tell Marie to throw herself out of the window, she rushes to the window like
an arrow from a bow, pushing aside violently those who
try to stop her. If she were found dead in the street,
who could say whether it were suicide or homicide?' . . .
' It is not necessary that an individual should present
the classic stages of the greater hypnotism in order
that he should be made to receive and to execute a
suggestion; the slightest and most superficial condition
suffices—simple fascination. The hypnotic under the
influence of suggestion is capable of becoming a dangerous lunatic of a new kind.' M. Luys also says, not
without a certain inconsistency, ' no one is obliged to
allow himself to be hypnotised, and the fact of having
delivered over to another even for a single instant his
moral liberty, suffices, in my opinion, to create a certain
measure of responsibility.' Dr. Luys is careful to recom-
mend to his pupils always to give the suggestion to the
persons whom they hypnotise not to allow themselves
to be hypnotised by anyone else, in order to avoid
such subjects becoming the subjects of exploitation by
interested persons.

This recommendation, highly significant as it is,

cannot be considered to be of any great value. A subject accustomed to be thrown into the hypnotic state cannot protect himself, and is at the mercy of any scoundrel or impostor who chooses to adopt the various methods of impressing the imagination which are the stock-in-trade of all hypnotisers. It is a mere idle fancy, easily disproved, that the hypnotiser has in himself any power special to him. All of M. Luys's subjects who passed under my hands, and indeed every subject who for many years has come under my notice, could be hypnotised, as I have already stated, by me or by anybody else whom they thought capable of hypnotising them; or by any object whatever—a candle, a bell, a spoon, a coin, or a tuning fork—to which they were taught to impute hypnotising power. In the substituted jargon of other schools this is called mesmeric power or magnetic power; all empty phrases for concealing the fact that the condition is one of a subjective character, capable of being induced by many kinds of external stimulus. M. Luys's porter, his ward servant, myself, and my friends proved to be as capable of hypnotising as Dr. Luys is himself. The dangers which he so vividly described are not therefore to be conjured by the simple expedient on which he relies. I may add that the newspapers in France abound with sad stories, and others are current in the hospitals of most distressing and grossly immoral results of this abominable practice of training responsible beings to resign their responsibility, and to become the passive agents of the will of others.

In connection with this part of the subject, and to throw a light on the active dangers associated with the practices of some of M. Luys's trained subjects, I think it right here to put on record the literal transcript of a letter I have received since reaching England from one of them (Jeanne), in which she describes the activities of herself and another subject of Dr. Luys's (Clarice), whom he introduced to me at his clinic, who is figured and described in his lectures, and to whom I have already referred :—

MONSIEUR LE DOCTEUR,—Ayant eu l'honneur Samedie dernier de servir de Sujet à une Seance d'hypnotism chez vous, Monsieur le Docteur, j'espère que vous voudrez bien m'excuser, Monsieur le Docteur, la liberte que je prends de vous faire parvenir une petite nomenclature—des expériences et des phénomènes—que Mr. le Dr. Luys obtien, depuis bien tot 7 ans, sur moi.

1. On obtien sur moi tres facilement —
   Les trois états classiques,
Léthargie, Catalepsie, Somnambulisme.
   En Léthargie.
Anestesie compléte.
Tous les différents effects et contracture—au contacte—
   des differents Metaux.
Les contractures Neuro-Musculaires.
Le jeu du Diaphragm.
   En Catalepsie.
Prise du regard—le point fixe—autométisme—les attitudes—Effects des Couleurs.

Suggestions par gestes.
Effects des Aimants.
Cessation du battement du poux.
Raideur cadaverique.
Somnambulisme.
Tous les phénomènes de l'hyperestesie de la peau.
Les attractions.
Effects de medicaments à distance.
Suggestion—instantanée et à écheance.
Changement de personalité !
Mneumonie.
Vision.
Vue *absolue* à travers tous les corps oppaques sans
   aucun secour des veux.
Double vue—transmission des pensées.

Voila Mr. le Docteur les phénomènes qu'on obtien très
facilement sur moi—*sans jamais les râter.*   Mr. Le Docteur Luys n'hésitera pas à le confirmer—d'ailleurs j'offre de
le prouver—quand on voudra.

Je travail en ce moment comme Sujet (passif) à la
Charité avec Mr. le Dr. Louys—et comme Sujet *active* avec
mes sujets—chez moi tous les jours de 2 heures a 6 heures—
et dans tous les Salons de la haute Aristocratie Parisienne
en soirée hypnotique ou Spirite.

Anciennements Mdlle. Clarice que Samedi Mr. le Docteur j'avais aperçue dans votre Salon—à été employée par
moi—pendant 8 mois *comme mon sujet.*   J'ai été force de
la conjedier pour un fait—assez serieux.   Cette petite dont
les aptitudes sont absolument aussi nules que le Cabotinage
est grande, profité des visites chez moi de quelques toutes
jeunes dames du plus grande monde qui dans l'après midi
venaient me consulter et naturellement en cachette de moi,
pour grossir ces gages de sujet, cette petite fille, sans

conscience vendai de la morphine au morphinomane et de l'opiome aux opiomanes, une de mes cliente, Mme. la Vicomtesse de . . . . devenue absolument opiomane par l'opiom procurai en secret par Clarice a manque payer cela de sa vie. Par un hasard ayant decouvert le verite j'ai mise Clarice immediatement à la porte. Voila pourquoi j'ai été desagreablement impressionée voyant cette triste personne singer avec aplond dans le salon de Mr. le Docteur tous ce qu'elle m'avais vu faire étant chez moi.

This letter will indicate some of the characteristics of the favoured patients and trained subjects of Dr. Luys, and a full investigation of the story, of which a corner of the veil is thus lifted, might be very useful in the interests of social morality.

Another ramification and extension of the proceedings at the Charité was disclosed to me by the presence at one of the sittings of a Madame W., who was appa-rently much interested in the proceedings, and presented me with her card and invited further acquaint-ance. I called with M. Cremière and found her installed at a library and reading room. It was the headquarters not only of profound hypnosis and the great hypnotism, but also of the new magic. Here I was introduced to the literature of occult science, and a ' methodical bibliography ' of the same was presented to me, being a critical study of the principal modern works on the subject by a group of occultists under the direction of Dr. Papus, President of the independent group of esoteric studies and director of ' L'Initiation. The book is interesting in itself, and all the more in-

L

teresting because Madame W. informed me that Papus,
or Dr. Papus, as he is described, is in fact M. Encausse,
whom I find described on the title page of Dr. Luys's
journal as 'Chef de Laboratoire de la Charité.'   To
those who wish to follow out the curious relationships
into which the Chef de Laboratoire of Dr. Luys has
entered, this little *bibliographie* will be singularly interesting.   It contains in itself a good deal of picturesque
and surprising information which makes it quite worth
the reading of anyone who is curious about the ramifications of so-called occultism, and the vagaries into
which the apostles of mesmerism and hypnotism often
allow themselves to wander.   The absolute key to occult
science is, it appears, to be found in the book entitled
'Le Tarot des Bohémiens, le plus Ancien Livre du
Monde à l'Usage Exclusive des Initiés,' par Papus.
Papus (Dr. Luys's Chef de Clinique) is also the author
of 'La Science des Mages, et ses Applications Théo-
riques et Pratiques.'   This is a little pamphlet, price
50 centimes.   In the press is announced to appear
immediately a series of books of which the first is
entitled, 'Erotique, comment on devient Fée.'   The
author not stated.

Under another rubric are the works on hypnotism.
Hypnotism, it is explained, studies the phenomena
produced in certain persons by physical or psychical
acts capable of fatiguing and surprising one of the
senses.   Hypnotisers differ from . magnetisers in that
they deny the existence of any fluid.   The 'Leçons

Cliniques' of Dr. Luys are warmly recommended, as
are those of Colonel de Rochas, who is described as one
of the rare French *savans* who occupy themselves in a
scientific manner with the forces, as yet little known,
of Nature and of man. Many new and very curious
discoveries on the relations of hypnotism and of the
ancient magnetism are brought to light in this work.
The journal called 'L'Initiation,' of which M. Papus
is the editor, deals with hypnotism, psychical force,
theosophy, kabala, gnostics, freemasonry and occult
sciences.[1]   To read through the whole of this catalogue
is like a nightmare.   It may be recommended to the
Psychical Society.   They will learn that, under the
name of 'telepathy' and of 'telepathic hallucination,'
certain French *savans* have approached the study of
the mysterious phenomena of the communication of
thought or of the vision of phantoms, and that 'this
study is part of occult science and of spiritism.'   Of
course I brought this and some of the literature away
with me; but as I understood that Madame W., the
presiding spirit of this Librairie du Merveilleux, could
also undertake to provide subjects for experiment, I
requested her assistance in that direction.   Most of
the available subjects, however, it appeared I already

---

[1] This gentleman has since honoured me with his abuse in the
Journal de Psychiatrie (edited by Dr. Luys).   The fact would not be
worth referring to except that M. Papus repeats the misstatement
that I experimented on persons whom Dr. Luys had discarded—the
truth being that two of them were actual patients, and all were introduced to me by Dr. Luys as his subjects of experiment.

had in hand, but she recommended us to apply to a Madame S., who, she said, was versed in the mysteries of *l'envoûtement*.

Here we came upon another and lower associated stratum. Madame S., who lived in the outer circle of Paris, occupied a little box of an apartment attached to some baths—bath-keeping being her principal employment and sorcery a by-occupation. The *mise en scène* was novel. She was a striking-looking person, with abundant and dishevelled grey locks. The room was pervaded by a number of black cats, of whom there were in all, I was told, nine who were her familiars. A toy demon held a prominent place on the wall, and a placard announced the price at which the magic cards were read and fortunes told. The tariff was moderate ; the *grand jeu* was, I think, 3 francs, the *petit jeu* 2 francs. Madame S. told us that it was not her business to practice *l'envoûtement*, but to remove its evil effects. In this she said she was very successful. She recounted to us several instances of great ladies and of actresses whom she had freed from its evil effects, as Madame W. had already told us. 'The process,' she explained, ' is very simple. Colonel de Rochas came to me to ask me to explain my power ; but he was not at all satisfied. I do it without magnetism, and that does not please him. I do it by the power of my will ; hatred, you know, is a power, and I oppose it. You hate anyone ; you get a spell thrown over them ; at a given time in the day or at a given place they suffer anguish, suffocation—they

waste away.   I remove the spell, and in three or four
sittings I cure them.   Send me anyone who has suffered
from *l'envoûtement* of Colonel de Rochas or anyone else
·and I can cure it.'   This lady's methods were crude and
suitable to her rank in life.   I do not pursue the matter
further ; but I refer to it as an instance and an evidence
of the abysses of folly and imposture to which the
persons whom I met at La Charité under the auspices of
Dr. Luys directed my footsteps.

The Position of Hypnotism in Therapeutics

The final question of the clinical physician and the
medical practitioner is the practical demand for the
definition of the position of hypnotism in its relation to
therapeutics.   I may, I think, take it as proved beyond
all reasonable doubt that the hypnotic condition is a
real and admitted clinical fact.   Setting aside all the
impostures, follies, and errors which have gathered
around it, brushing away the fantastic halo of clairvoyance, telepathic and visional communication, transference of thought or sensation across space, or by contact and externalisation of sensation, as pure fallacies,
fancies, or frauds, we have still the solid basis of the
subjective condition of artificially induced sleep and
heightened suggestibility.   What use then, if any, can
be made of the power of suggestion under these circumstances as a curative agent ?   In reply to this question
I will adduce chiefly the evidence of Dr. Luys, Dr.

Charcot, Dr. Babinski, and M. Ballet, analysing the results of long years of clinical experiment on a vast number of subjects in Paris and in Nancy.   M. Babinski discusses the subject very carefully in a lecture which he gave at the Salpêtrière on June 23, 1891.[1]   He opens his lecture very frankly with the following statement:—'At the Salpêtrière, without at all objecting to hypnotism as a weapon of the therapeutic arsenal, it is considered that its indications are limited, and that this mode of cure can hardly be applied with success except in hysteria.'   'In any case it may,' he considers, 'be affirmed (p. 23) that the greater part of the symptoms which have been cured by this method arise from and belong to that neurosis.'   'Hypnotism,' he further says, 'may, it must be admitted, serve in the treatment of hysterical manifestations, but it must also be acknowledged that even in affections of this class, hypnotic practice does not give brilliant results.'

From the therapeutic point of view he groups hysterics into two distinct classes.   To the first belong the great number of hysterical persons who are not capable of being hypnotised, however much trouble is taken with them.   Some of these patients are no doubt subject to the very old-fashioned influence of suggestion in the waking state.   Such people have always been

---

[1] *Hypnotisme et Hystérie : du Rôle de l'Hypnotisme en Thérapeutique.*   Leçon faite à la Salpêtrière le 23 Juin 1891, par J. Babinski, médecin des hôpitaux, ancien chef de clinique des maladies nerveuses à la Faculté.   Paris: G. Masson, 1891.

susceptible to cure by bread pills and distilled water
and by the 'rapid' influence of electrotherapy, hydro-
therapy, &c. In the second class are the hysterics,
persons who can be hypnotised, and these present
numerous varieties. Some of them, especially those
subject to hysterical neuralgia and cutaneous hyperæs-
thesia, are very rebellious to suggestion, and in others
only a partial and very inadequate result can be
obtained. In some cases of hysterical contraction of
the limbs suggestion gives relief, but it has to be
renewed from day to day, sometimes five or six times
a day, and the patient is very liable to relapse. In
a very few cases a gradual and definite amelioration
is obtained, as in one case of hysterical muscular contraction and coxalgia which Dr. Babinski is able to
quote. 'Finally,' he asks himself after many years
of study and experience as *chef de clinique des
maladies nerveuses* and as an hospital physician, who
has constantly observed the cases at the Salpêtrière,
' does the field of action of hypnotism pass beyond
the domain of hysteria ? ' His final conclusion, which
he italicises at the close of his address, is that it
is justifiable to say, and he is authorised to conclude
that outside of hysteria there does not exist a single
affection capable of being notably modified by hypnotism, or at least that the contrary is not proved, for
the cases published with that object are far from
being demonstrative. Of course the opposite thesis is
maintained by M. Bernheim, but after the close analysis

to which Dr. Babinski subjects the cases published by Dr. Bernheim in his two books on psychotherapy and suggestion, there remains very little which can be accepted as substantial

In addition to bodily diseases some alienist physicians have alleged that mental maladies may be cured by hypnotism.   Here again we may take the results of competent French alienists who have given a practical trial to this method.   M. Magnan authorises the statement that experiments made on the treatment of insanity by hypnotism at the Bureau de l'Admission during three years had given no appreciable result, while M. Bernheim himself recognises that the domain of mental alienation is the most rebellious to suggestion.   Dr. Forel, of Zürich, is not less positive in his conclusions. He says [1] :—' Insane ideas have never been modified in any patient.   Even those whom I succeeded in hypnotising, in rendering anæsthesic and amnesic, whom I made realise post-hypnotic suggestions, refused to accept any suggestion opposed to their insane ideas.   I never succeeded in influencing the course of true melancholia (I do not speak of hysteric melancholia) by suggestion ; at most I was able sometimes to produce sleep, and in one case to hasten convalescence.'   M. Briand, Chief Physician of the Asile of Villejuif, said on the same occasion :—' I have many times attempted to send to sleep the insane and delirious who presented no hysteric

---

[1] *Premier Congrès International de l'Hypnotisme*, p. 155.   Paris : Octave Doin, Editeur, 1890.

taint, but I was never fortunate enough to obtain any result.' If this is so in France, the results are likely to be at least as negative in Great Britain, where the population is undoubtedly much less susceptible to suggestion.

HYPNOTIC SUGGESTION BEFORE THE LAW

It has been alleged that suggestion and somnambulism may have considerable value in unmasking certain crimes to which the tribunals of justice have not hitherto been able to attribute their true character. This thesis has been especially maintained by M. Liégeois[1] and by M. A. Voisin,[2] but with all his goodwill and with all his research M. Liégeois has not been able to bring forward one single example in which suggestion has been shown to play any part in the production of a crime brought before a court of law.   I refer those who are interested to the excellent analysis of the work of M. Liégeois by Gilbert Ballet.[3]

There is only one case on record in which a distinct declaration has been made by a medical man of evidence that crime has been committed by a hypnotised person

---

[1] *De la Suggestion et du Somnambulisme dans leurs Rapports avec la Jurisprudence et la Médecine Légale.* Paris, 1889. *Comptes Rendus du Congrès de l'Hypnotisme,* 1889.

[2] *Revue de l'Hypnotisme* de Juin 1891.

[3] *Les Suggestions Hypnotiques au Point de Vue Médico-legale.* Par Gilbert Ballet, Professor Agrégé à la Faculté de Médecine, Médecin de l'Hôpital St.-Antoine. Paris: G. Masson.

under the influence of suggestion.   It is the case which
M. Voisin records in the ' Revue de l'Hypnotisme' here
cited, in which, as he reports, a woman accomplished
numerous thefts at a large shop when in a state of automatism and under suggestion which had been imposed
upon her when hypnotised.   M. Voisin states that he demonstrated the complete irresponsibility of this woman,
who was set at liberty, while the three actual authors
of the crime were punished.   Dr. Voisin referred also
to this case, in my presence, at the Bournemouth
meeting of the British Medical Association.   If it be
fully verified, it may claim to rank as a case in which
the theory of post-hypnotic suggestion has been of
use for justice.   It would be the only case thus far
noted.   But where are the legal documents of this
case, the magistrates' report, and the depositions?
Until we have these before us we can decide nothing
as to its authority.   They have been pressingly asked
for, but I am not aware that they have been produced.   That hypnotism may and does lead to crime
in respect to the abuse by hypnotic operators of the
person of the hypnotised subject is beyond question,
and possibly the cases may be more numerous than
published records can prove ; but to the question which
we are now putting, of the influence of suggestion in
producing crime as the automatic act of the subject, or
as the result of deferred suggestion, there is no affirma-
tive answer forthcoming upon evidence adduced.   Still
less is there any proof that the doctrine of hypnotic

suggestion has in any case been of value for the purposes of justice.

Finally, I pass to the domain of surgery and obstetrics. Here we are on more positive ground, and I shall quote the words of Dr. Luys [1]—always disposed to give the largest interpretation to the evidence of the usefulness of hypnotism—as to its relative inutility in these positive departments of medical and surgical art.

SURGICAL APPLICATION

'At the first appearance of hypnotism, when Braid had shown that hypnotised subjects are insensitive to external stimuli, surgeons conceived the idea of using this method for the performance of certain operations; in fact, a certain number among them had the opportunity of testing it with a certain amount of advantage; but since the wonderful discovery of chloroform, these attempts so far as concerns surgical anæsthesia have been justly abandoned.

'At the present time the application of hypnotism to surgical therapeutics is of absolutely no account, since it concerns only the limited number of persons comprised in the class of hypnotisable subjects. It must, however, be said that if this class of subjects should, by the employment of new methods, become more numerous, it is possible that in certain cases one might practise

[1] *Applications Thérapeutiques de l'Hypnotisme.*   Par le Dr. J. Luys.   Paris : Imprimerie F. Leve, 17 Rue Casette.   1889.

fascination, and thus obtain an artificial anæsthesia, the duration of which might be prolonged without any ill effects. In the present state of things, when a small operation is to be done upon any of our hypnotic subjects, an abscess is to be opened, a foreign body to be extracted or one or more teeth to be drawn, I do not hesitate to hypnotise the subject and to hand him over to the surgeon. It happens to me frequently enough to have a certain number of subjects with teeth to be drawn. I place them in the condition of lucid somnambulism, I address myself to the dentists of the Charité, who examine the mouth at leisure, and extract the diseased teeth ; whilst the subject, insensible throughout, on waking has no recollection of the operation he has undergone, and is quite astonished to find his extracted teeth in his hand.'

APPLICATION OF HYPNOTISM IN THE DOMAIN OF OBSTETRICS

Dr. Luys further writes :—' The practice of hypnotism as applied to the art of midwifery has not yet yielded very satisfactory results. You may read on this subject a very interesting work written by Dr. Auvard, who sums up in a very conscientious way all that is known about this question. I have only had one single fact of this kind to record, and it does not seem of a nature to encourage hypnotic experiments in this special province. Last year I had in my wards a young hypnotic woman whom I had kept till the last day of her pregnancy in order to give her the benefit of lethargic anæsthesia at the time of her confinement. When the pains came on she was hypnotised and placed in a condition of lethargy ; but this procedure proved perfectly useless, for the intensity of the labour pains was such that they brought about the natural awakening of the patient, and we were obliged to have recourse to chloroform to finish the delivery.'

To sum up, I may venture to quote my own conclusions as stated recently in the ' Nineteenth Century ' : To me the so-called cures by hypnotism seem to rank in precisely the same class as those of the faith-curer.

The hypnotic *endormeur* is very well able to explain the miracles of faith-cure by the light of his own experience. They result, as he explains accurately, from the reaction of mind on body, the effects of imagination, of self-suggestion, or of suggestion from without. Those who benefit by them are especially the fervent and the enthusiastic, the vividly imaginative, the mentally dependent, and, above all, the hysterical—male or female. But clearly the faith-curer may retort upon the hypnotiser that they are brothers in their therapeutic results, if not in their faith and philosophy. The one can work about the same percentage of cures as the other, and no more ; and the intervening apparatus, whether of magnets, mirrors or grottos, only serve to affect the imagination, and to supply the necessary ' external stimulus.'

To this category also belong the long series of thousands of asserted cures of people who now wear what they are pleased to call magnetic belts, or who used to wear magnetic rings and believed they were cured by the Perkins tractors of wood or iron— people who are the prey of quacks of all ages and in all countries.

One essential fact is, it appears to me, that no new faculty has ever yet been developed in any of these hypnotics. The frauds of clairvoyance, spirit perceptions, gifts of language, slate-writing, spirit-writing, far-sight, 'communication across space,' 'transfer of mental impressions,' of the development of any new sense or the ghost of a new sense, remain, now as ever, for the most part demonstrable frauds, or perhaps, in a few cases, self-deceptions. At the Salpêtrière, at Nancy and wherever the facts have been impartially and critically examined, this has been the result. A similar outcome is obtained by my recent tests of the subjects of the Charité and the Ecole Polytechnique. It will, I suppose, be too much to expect that we shall hear no more of the 'New Mesmerism,' but it will be easy for anyone to reduce it to its true dimensions by similar experiments.

Finally; as to the practical question, which has perhaps a greater interest for the sociologist and the physician than any which have suggested themselves up to this point. Since the hypnotist faith-curer of the hospital ward and the priestly faith-curer of the grotto are in truth utilising the same human elements and employing cognate resources, although masked by a different outward garb, we may ask ourselves which of them can claim the greater successes and which does the least harm ?

So far as I can see, the balance is in favour of the faith-curer of the chapel and the grotto. The results at least are proportionately as numerous, and they are more rapid. Numerically there are, I incline to believe, more faith-cures at Lourdes than there are 'suggestion-cures' in the Salpêtrière or the Charité. So far as hypnotism is good for anything as a curative agent, its sphere is, as we have seen, limited by Charcot, Féré, Babinski and all the most trustworthy medical observers in Paris, to the relief of functional disorders and symptoms in hysterical patients. The Nancy school put their pretensions higher ; but anyone who will analyse for himself the Nancy reputed cases of cure, or who will study Babinski's able analysis of them, will easily satisfy himself that such claims are not valid. As to the use of 'suggestion' as an anæsthetic substitute of chloroform for operation purposes, that 'suggestion' dates back beyond the times of Esdaile and of Elliotson. It has been given up and fallen into disuse because of its unreliability and limited application. It is now seriously proposed to use hypnotism for 'tooth-drawing,' for the treatment of drunkards, and of school children. The proposition is self-condemned. To enable a dentist to draw a tooth painlessly, the average man or woman is, by a series of sittings, to be reduced to the state of a trained automaton ; which happily is only possible in the case of a very small proportion. The criminal courts have seen enough of hypnotic dentists. As to the 'suggestion' cure of drunkards or the 'suggestion' treatment of backward or naughty children, systematic and intelligent suggestion is what every clergyman, every doctor, and every schoolmaster tries to carry out in such cases and often effects successfully and in a better form than the degrading one of hypnotism. Moreover, for drunkenness it is, so far as my inquiries go, a disappointing failure.

If a striking effect is to be produced by an apparatus calculated to affect the imagination powerfully, the faith-curer of the grotto has this advantage over the *endormeur* of the platform or the hospital. He does not intrude his own personality and train his patient to subject his mental *ego* to that of his 'operator.' The 'mesmeriser' seeks to dominate his subject; he weakens the will power, which it is desirable to strengthen, and aims at becoming the master of a slave. I do not need further to emphasise the dangers of this practice.

The faith-curer of the grotto strengthens the weaker individuality. He plays upon the spring of self-suggestion. The patient is told to believe that he will be cured, to wish it fervently and he shall be cured. So far as he is cured, he returns to his home perhaps a better and a stronger man, and his cure is quite as real and likely to be quite as lasting as if he had become the puppet of a hypnotiser. The experiments of the Salpêtrière have served to enable us to analyse more clearly the nature of faith cures generally, and they have thrown a ray of light on a series of phenomena of human automatism never before studied so clearly or philosophically, but they have added practically little, if anything, to our curative resources. It is hardly to be set down to their discredit that they have incidentally favoured the reign of the platform hypnotiser and the vagaries of the subjects at La Charité; that result is their misfortune rather than their fault, though it is a grave misfortune. But the intervention of authority might now, and I hope will, cut short the absurdities of these practices, and put an end to some social mischiefs which have fastened on to them and hang on to their skirts. Thus much as to the medical question. To the student of ' psychological phenomena ' it is of great interest to note how successive functions may be separately abolished as the brain is partially set to sleep, and in what exaggerated forms the remaining activities may be brought into action when restraining self-consciousness is stilled. The vulgar, too, may find an ignoble amusement in the antics of these drinkers of petroleum and vinegar, of these seers of visions and in the semi-idiotic postures and proceedings of the hypnotised mannikin, just as they do in a *fantocchini* show. But against such philosophic satisfactions and vulgar amusements must be set the avowed as well as the unconfessed mischiefs wrought by hypnotic experiments; and who can doubt that these outbalance any apparent good result ?

M

GROPINGS AFTER THE
SUPERNATURAL

THERE have always been persons who claimed the gift
or distinction of conversing with spirits. Science, with
its rigorous analysis and its exact methods of proof, has
made an end of many imaginary beings. Nymphs,
fauns, river gods, fairies, brownies, kelpies, and spirits
of every kind have fallen out of belief; but communications from the unseen world, it is alleged, still reach
our world, adapting themselves to the new methods of
experimental philosophy. Ghosts now write letters,
and show a disposition to suffer themselves to be
photographed. We should be loth to deride such
gropings after the supernatural. Human curiosity cannot be repelled from trying to peer through the
curtain which covers the world beyond the grave.
Those who have thrown off a belief in the traditional
views of religion are sometimes moved to seek a con-
firmation of the spirit world through experiments
pursued in a quasi-scientific manner. We do not say
that all those who take to spiritualism are sceptics, but
the tendency generally indicates a decaying faith in
revealed religion.

Paris—long the capital of religious scepticism—
seems to be at present the head-quarters of the
clairvoyants, spiritualists, and other mystics, who endeavour to establish a familiar intercourse between the
living and the dead. A well-known journalist (Mr.
Stead) has confided to the public some visitations
which he has had from the spirits. ' Julia,' the shade
of a defunct American journalist (whom we should
much desire to interview, and who might with advantage be subjected to ' test,' as were the subjects of La
Charité), has imparted to him not only information
about business matters, of which the dead might be
expected to take little care, but also details about the
spiritual condition after death, and Mr. Stead has communicated them to some English bishops, who are
presumably experts in such matters. These dignitaries,
we are told, consider ' Julia's' revelations to be worthy
of attention. Apparently none of these interesting
confidences have as yet been printed for the edification
of the profane vulgar.

Mr. Stead has been visited by what may be called
spiritual influxes. His hand is moved involuntarily to
write things new even to himself. (See Appendix p. 210.)
He has a friend whom he has got to write involuntarily a
confession of some events which a man of ordinary reticence
would have left untold. Mr. Stead is disposed to think
that a murderer might, under the promptings of his
better self, reveal the crimes which he had committed;
but then some criminals, he naïvely observes, have no

better self. We agree with Mr. Maskelyne that there
is no use laying down a test for the spiritualists any
more than for the clairvoyants. To begin with they
always object to it, and when the tests are rigidly
enforced by men of a scientific cast of mind, the wonder-
workers always fail. How often, for example, have the
clairvoyants or ghost-seers been asked to read some
document or tell the number of a bank note carefully
locked up, and always in vain ? Sometimes they offer
the excuse that spirits cannot, or will not, tell everything. Very likely, it is said, the shades do not care
whether physiologists believe in them or not, and will
not condescend to answer impertinent questions or to
suffer cross-examinations of a detective character. You
must take what they tell you in the way they tell it to
you. The spiritualists have never told us anything worth
knowing, and, what is worse, they are in hopeless dis-
agreement with one another. Will common sense not
teach people that, if there really were a channel of
intercourse between the living and the dead, many a
message would come from friends gone before, of serious
and weighty import instead of trifles and ineptitudes
which have a suspicious resemblance to echoes of the
thoughts of the living ?

Swedenborg, the prince of visionaries, whose ac-
counts of the unseen world are circumstantial enough,
manages to exclude rivals, for he declares that the
spirits of the dead cannot converse with the living, and
he himself was, by the special ordination of God, made

an exception to this rule. Occasionally the Swedish mystic allowed spirits to see through his eyes, and he tells us that the spirits of fraudulent tradespeople moved his hand to make him steal articles in the shops. Scientific psychologists treat these as subjective feelings, dependent upon deranged conditions of the nervous system, in most cases accompanied by other symptoms of disease. Mr. Stead can only explain his own abnormal sensations, mental impulses, and involuntary muscular actions as the result of the influx of spirits. Accepting this as ' a working hypothesis,' he assures us he is acting in an honest, and, he hopes, a scientific manner. But there are many things, both in disease and health, which are not yet fully explicable by any hypothesis. An impatient desire to have a hypothesis has led science into countless errors. A literary man, whose mind has had no training in physiology, is likely to go astray in such inquiries. I venture to advise Mr. Stead to subject all his symptoms to the analysis of a skilful physician, instead of hurriedly reducing vague nervous sensations into copy for periodical publications.

'THE ETERNAL GULLIBLE'

THE CONFESSIONS OF A PROFESSIONAL 'HYPNOTIST'[1]

THAT genial old sceptic, Montaigne, summed up his criticism of life in the terse aphorism, 'L'homme se pipe.' Man cheats himself even more than he is cheated. Gullibility springs eternal in the human breast ; in the evolution of the race other feelings and beliefs wither away like organs which have lost their use ; this alone abides with us as an inalienable birth-right. In the immortal words of Robert Macaire, ' Tout passe ; mais les badauds ne passeront jamais.' In the eternal gullible, which is a primary constituent in the nature of ' this foolish-compounded clay, man,' lies the whole secret of the success of quackery of all kinds. This chronic disease of the human mind is subject to periodical exacerbations under the influence of what appear to be pandemic waves of credulity. At the present moment we are passing through such a phase of occultation of common sense, and hypnotism, spiritualism, telepathy, 'spookism' in its various manifestations, Mahatmism, Matteism, and intellectual fungi of a like

[1] Reprinted from the *Century Illustrated Monthly Magazine*, October 1894.

kind, flourish in rankest luxuriance in the minds of men and women, some of whom in other respects give evidence of more than average intelligence.

To prevent misconception, it may be well for me to repeat here that I do not deny the physical facts of hypnotism and its heteronyms. It is the interpretation of them, put forth by some hierophants of the cult, that I consider erroneous. I fully admit that, under the influence of certain psychological stimuli, persons whose nervous system is ill-balanced, or at best in a condition of unstable equilibrium, readily pass into a state which we may, if we choose, call 'hypnotic sleep.' In view of the doubtful connotation which, owing to unsavoury associations, the word 'hypnotism' has acquired, I prefer to designate the condition here referred to as 'Braidism,' after the name of its most philosophical exponent, the late Mr. Braid of Manchester. I think there can be no doubt that the condition is mental and purely subjective, but there must also be a pathological coefficient on which the susceptibility of the patient to the so-called 'hypnotic influence' depends. As to the nature of this coefficient, or of the condition which it underlies, we are at present in the dark; there are unfortunately still some riddles in medicine of which the solution has yet to be discovered, and this which we call 'Braidism,' or 'hypnotism,' is to that extent one of them. However, we are at least sure that there is nothing miraculous about this condition, no 'magnetism,' no 'efflux of will-power,' no added function of the organism or new power of mind, nothing, in short, preternatural—unless it be the credulity of those who accept them as signs and wonders. The hypnotist counts for nothing in the matter, except as an object inanimate or animate affecting the imagination of the subject, who is always self-hypnotised.

A chief obstacle in the way of the scientific investigation of hypnotism is the difficulty of finding any solid footing in the quagmire of error, self-delusion, and downright imposture in which this *ignis fatuus* of the human intellect lives and moves and has its being. Even in the hands of medical men of high character the proportion of truth to mere error is as Falstaff's halfpenny worth of bread to his intolerable deal of sack. As for the hypnotism and the crystal-gazing of the drawing-room and of the public platform it is, so far as the 'subjects' are concerned, of imposture all compact. I have already shown how Dr. Luys's subjects, in their own words, 'gulled' him, and how sadly he played the part of dupe and decoy. If such things be possible in the green wood of an intellect originally trained to scientific observation, what is likely to happen in the dry sticks and shavings of half-educated, wholly uncritical, and superstitious minds ready to take fire at the slightest spark of the mysterious? The fact is that without specially trained 'subjects' hypnotism could not exist. Even Charcot had to put his chief subjects through a long course of training to fit them for his public displays at the Salpêtrière. In accordance with a fundamental law of political economy, the demand has created the supply; hence that curious product of our latter day *Aberglaube*, the professional 'subject,' has come to be. Of the nature and significance of this 'sign of the times' something may be gathered from the tale I am about to unfold.

A year or two ago I was the recipient of the confessions of a professional subject, who had come to see the error of his ways, or, as I fear is more probable, finding his occupation gone (for your 'subject' loses his commercial value by over-use), was not unwilling—for a consideration—to unfold the story of his 'professional' life. He was sent to me by the editor of 'Truth,' into whose sympathetic ear he had first poured the story of his career as a *corpus vile* of pseudo-scientific experiment. The confessions of this ingenuous youth are amusing and instructive, though, as in most confidences of the kind, the light is thrown strongly on the sins and shortcomings of others, while the penitent's own peccadillos are left in shadow. They are, unfortunately, too long to give in full, but I may say that the original documents submitted to me prove that in the most noted hypnotic exhibitions given on public platforms, at the Aquarium in London, and other places of amusement, the performers, both hypnotisers and hypnotised, are, almost without exception, conscious humbugs going through a pre-arranged 'show,' and, to quote the *vates sacer* of the Heathen Chinee, 'the same with intent to deceive.' In the inner circles of the music halls, the 'line' of the professional subject is, I find, as well recognised as that of the contortionist, or any other variety of mountebank. He is engaged in the usual way, and his earnings are proportionate to his professional skill—that is, to his power of gulling the groundlings. Nor, taking into account the disagreeable experiences which he has to go through, can it be said that his line of business is particularly remunerative. His muscles must be under extraordinary control; his palate must be disciplined to tolerate, and his stomach to retain, such delicacies as castor-oil, mustard, Cayenne pepper, paraffin, and ipecacuanha; and he must bear pain with the impassive stoicism of an Indian brave. It is clear that a professional subject must not only be born, but must be made, and to the making of him there must go an amount of trouble worthy of a better cause. His professional equipment must include some measure of histrionic ability, as, in his time, he has many parts to play. Above all, he must, like the Roman augurs, cultivate a command of countenance which shall prevent his laughing outright in the faces of his dupes.

My interesting penitent allowed me the privilege of seeing his business correspondence, from which the story of his professional life, from year to year, can be extracted. According to these documents, his first introduction to mesmerism was at St. James's Hall. This important event is best described in his own words :

When I first went to the above show, I was sitting

among the audience when a mesmerised subject rushed up
to me, and said the place was on fire.   He tried to pull me
away from my seat, but I would not go, till at last
Mr. ——[1] came up and awakened him.   As I was leaving
the building, that subject came up to me, and apologised
for the trouble he had occasioned me.   He asked me
whether I would have a ticket for the following evening ;
he gave me a ticket, and I came again the following
evening.   When I saw him again, he asked me if I believed
in it ; I answered yes.   He asked me if I thought I could
do the same ; I said no.   He said he would teach me if I
liked.

My penitent has been endowed by Nature with a
countenance which resembles Pindar's verses in being
'significant to the initiated.'   I am therefore not surprised that he was quickly recognised by the sympathetic
intuition of a kindred spirit as one born to hypnotic
greatness.   In his modest diffidence as to his capacity
in that direction we may recognise the 'unconsciousness'
which, according to Carlyle, is a distinguishing attribute
of the highest genius.   An appointment was made for
the following morning at an address in the classic region
of Drury Lane, and there the neophyte received his first
lesson in the mysteries of his art.

When I came there I saw half a dozen other young
fellows who went through all sorts of tricks.   Mr. ——
was not present.   Then he [presumably the amiable subject
who had discerned the latent possibilities in our friend's

---

[1] I have all the names as they stand in the original documents,
but omit them here.

expressive physiognomy] told me to sit down and close my eyes and pretend to fall asleep, and he stuck a needle in my arm and asked if it hurt much. I said no. After a few more tricks, like falling from my chair, I was asked to come up for one week for 15s. Being without employment, I accepted. When I came up for the first time on the stage, the mesmerist tried to put me to sleep, but I did not [sic], as I was afraid.

Some further tuition was necessary, and for a short time the candidate was not trusted to do anything on the stage beyond going to sleep, in the meantime learning different tricks at the seminary in Drury Lane. He was an apt pupil, and very soon he was able to do several things which he had been taught, such as ' laugh, cry, smoking tallow candles, and being fireman.' The rapid progress of our hero is proved by the fact that apparently within a couple of weeks of his being taken in hand by the principal of the Drury Lane Academy aforesaid, whom he calls his ' agent and trainer,' he, in his own words, ' went through catelepsy [sic], oil-drinking, needle, and all other tricks.'

In course of time we find our now fully fledged ' subject,' whom I will call L., performing with a well-known professor of hypnotism at the Royal Aquarium and elsewhere. He seems to have been at first taken on trial, but having gone to sleep, been pierced with needles, and drunk a glass of ' paraffin mixture ' to the satisfaction of the mesmerist, he was engaged as a regular ' subject ' at 1l. 15s. a week. By this operator L. was, in his own words, ' put in catelepsy ' [sic], and had two fellows laid across him, with the master himself on top. In fact, so promising a subject was he considered that he was selected by the 'professor' for private demonstrations. Having been seen talking to gentlemen in the Aquarium, he received a serious caution from his employer not to reveal the fact that he was pretending to be under mesmeric influence, and not 'to go to anybody's private house,' presumably on his own account. He speaks of having worked eighteen months with his employer at different places, such as the Agricultural Hall, Bow, Sanger's, and Shoreditch, besides the Royal Aquarium. During this engagement his stomach was put to some severe tests, as he had at various times to eat tallow candles, cigarettes, raw onions, &c., and to drink a variety of 'vile concoctions.'

L. next became connected with another 'professor,' with whom he performed at the Aquarium, giving 'two shows a day,' going through 'the usual tricks.' The 'professor's' style seems to have been of the robust order ; he is described as throwing 'the subjects most unmercifully about, and especially the bad ones.' At the request of a doctor a penknife was on one occasion stuck into L.'s arm. The following newspaper report of the 'show' at the Aquarium is interesting in view of L.'s own statement as to his previous appearances on the same stage :

The subjects were very much of the same class of men that Mr. —— operated upon, and in some instances they were challenged as to whether they had not appeared with ——, *an assertion which they stoutly denied.*

At one time Succi, the fasting man, travelled with them, and he also appears to have been smitten with the noble ambition to become a mesmerist. He tried his prentice hand on L., who, being nothing if not accommodating, allowed him to succeed, to the great disgust of his employer, who feared that Succi might set up as a rival showman in the hypnotic line.

L. next appears as an instructor in the art and mystery of hypnotism. Under his tuition his pupil soon blossomed into a 'professor,' and gave some successful public exhibitions of his mesmeric influence, which led to an engagement at the Royal Aquarium. There he and his *fidus Achates* remained eight months, demonstrating the wonders of hypnotism to an admiring public. At these performances our poor fakir of a 'subject' had to put six bonnet pins through his cheeks, drink any amount of paraffin mixture, go twice a day through 'catalepsy, and imitate Samson the strong man.'

With Dr. ——, another member of the hypnotic fraternity, our hero became acquainted through an advertisement in the 'Era.' On calling upon the mesmerist he saw three country lads going through what may be called the goose step of mesmerism and hypnotism. L., however, who had got more insight into the inwardness of hypnotism than most of his employers, advised his master to get London subjects, who might be supposed, in the classic words of Sam Weller, to be 'up to snuff and a pinch or two over,' and warned him against the danger of his show being wrecked by the stupidity of country subjects. His engagement with Dr. —— does not seem to have been very brilliant in point of profit. The terms were, however, subsequently raised on L.'s giving assurance that he was used to the 'needle business.' But the interesting partnership was dissolved because although the subject had all the heavy work to do he could obtain no further increase of pay. The letters before me show the extremely businesslike way in which these public hypnotists arrange for a proper supply of subjects, who travel with them as regular members of the 'company,' and have to give satisfactory assurance before being engaged as to the quality and extent of their powers.

L.'s advice to his employer was thoroughly sound; it would be to the last degree dangerous for a professor of hypnotism to trust to local talent for his public displays. A proof of this occurred while L. was at Birmingham. The 'Dr.' usually took the precaution of giving the oil-drinking and 'all the heavy and difficult things' to L. to do. One night, however, he tried to make one of his country subjects take the oil, but the latter refused, and a scene was prevented only by L.'s ingeniously creating a diversion which changed a commencing hiss into applause.

Another 'professor' he first met at the Middlesex Music Hall, where, with an eye to possible business, he gave the hypnotist his professional card. The result is seen in the following letter, dated October 16, 1891:

I have just dropped across your card. I am going to open at Greenwich on Boxing day. I want two subjects.

I should like to know whether you are used to the oil and needle business and can do *catelepsy*. Please let me know by return.

Apparently L. was able to satisfy this eminent performer as to his exceptional talents as a subject to such an extent that he was eager to secure another subject equally gifted. This is shown by the following extract from a letter dated December 20 :

Yours to hand. If the other fellow is also used to the needle and oil he can come as well. I will give you each thirty shillings for the seven days. Be at the Hall at 3 o'clock sharp. Do not disappoint me. Inclosed find two tickets.

P.S.—Learn a good comic song if you can.

The postscript shows that in addition to his powers as a fakir, and to his general histrionic capacity, the subject who wishes to reach the highest pinnacle in his profession must, as Goethe said, ' develop his powers in every possible direction,' and all for thirty shillings a week. This particular ' professor ' ' made impressions without talking to the subjects,' but as a man of forethought who left nothing to accident, he was careful to give instructions beforehand as to what was to be done every night. L.'s powers of endurance were somewhat severely tested by an inquiring doctor, who stuck a penknife into his leg, and tested him by lighting a match under his eye, and by ' rubbing the eyeballs.'

Here our subject takes us into his confidence, and reveals one of the tricks of the trade, for he says, 'having the eyes turned up, we cannot see anything.' If this device succeeded in deceiving any member of the medical profession, it could have been only by the operation of faith, which not only moves mountains, but seems to deprive otherwise observant men of the use of their senses. Truly the hypnotic showman and his acolytes, finding people so willing to be deceived, may almost be forgiven for saying with Autolycus: 'Ha! ha! What a fool Honesty is, and Trust, his sworn brother, a very simple gentleman!'

L.'s next employer was an 'editor,' who had become acquainted with him at the Royal Aquarium during one of his previous performances there. He is said to have been very sceptical at first, but L. convinced him—an interesting example of the faith born of the will to believe, of which theologians tell us. Behold now the able editor reincarnated as a professional hypnotist, giving exhibitions at Blackfriars Road, Brentwood, the Metropolitan Music Hall, and at private houses. This new avatar seems, however, to have been a failure. To quote the words of L., 'He did not seem to succeed, so took on private pupils, which he is training now,' a view of the place of the teacher of hypnotism which may be compared with Lord Beaconsfield's description of critics as men who have failed in literature and art.

L.'s next engagement was with a lady hypnotist, with whom, to use his own words, he 'gave different

N

shows at all sorts of clubs and music halls.' They were also engaged for the Royal Aquarium, which seems to be the San Carlo of such exhibitions; but here the professional jealousy of a rival hypnotist interfered with the arrangement, and they had to ' seek fresh woods and pastures new.' The fair mesmerist would seem to have been the object of considerable jealousy on the part of her male rivals. Miss ——, we are assured, was at first a believer in her own possession of a mysterious mesmeric power, but L. opened her eyes on the subject, a useful part he was well qualified to play. The following extracts from the business correspondence of this lady are interesting, as showing the care that has to be taken in selecting for these exhibitions subjects that can be trusted to go through the usual rites without indecorous levity, and without mistaking the situation.

To-day my arrangements have been completed, and am now under the orders of —— [a well-known theatrical agent], so that at any time he may be pleased I shall have to appear, so according to your promise I want you to procure about six easy subjects to begin with. I should be pleased if you could forward their addresses. (Only men who could be surely relied upon, I mean that would come upon the stage for sure, and temperate.) For each man I will allow you two shillings ; their wages will be settled by my agent to-morrow, which I shall see to being liberal.

Sorry I could not write as promised on Saturday, but nothing really definite was arranged concerning the men's wages. The latest desire of Mr. —— being that on Wed.

he would like to see just two of the *smartest* subjects
obtainable—must be 'gentlemanly' with a view to their
further engagement—he has some idea of my getting up
quite a novel show (with perhaps two men only). Now if
you care to make one find the other (don't forget he must
be smart and good-looking—that's the order), I should
prefer a cataleptic subject if this is agreeable, please to be
at ——'s office —— at 1.45 sharp on Wed. morning.

The lady's style is a little incoherent, and she
shows an ultra-feminine contempt for punctuation; but
she manages to make it clear that she wants a
particular kind of goods delivered punctually and in
sound condition. L. seems to have been successful in
finding the class of subject required, for on August 7,
1891, Miss —— writes:

Thanks for your prompt reply with addresses. I will
allow you to judge them, as to subjects I *suppose them to
have been controled before*. I don't know how soon I may
require them—of course with you.

From the stipulation as to the subjects having been
controlled before, the lady seems to have been somewhat distrustful of her own powers, but her confidence
in her leading subject, Mr. L., was evidently complete.
In another letter we find her asking for subjects 'not
too well known,' and especially bargaining for a supply
of 'decent young men' that she can depend upon.
This difficulty in connection with professional subjects
—that they may become too well known—recurs more
than once in Miss ——'s letters; thus she adds a
postscript to one, to the following effect:

N.B.—I hope they are not too easily recognisable at the Aquarium. I should like their names and addresses.

The following letter is another example of the careful way in which the arrangements for these performances are made beforehand :

The gentlemen would have to be at the hall at 6.30 sharp. For this occasion I will give them 4s. each—and this will in all probability lead to a permanent engagement at once,—for which the proprietor has already undertaken to pay 5s. a turn each and every occasion, being, as it is a music hall, one half-hour only—it is a stage rather bigger than at Aquarium, and being rather a decent place, of course *I must this time be sure of their turning up.* Now could you get about eight men, one half cataleptic, for this occasion ? *Write by return* as there is so little time—only if agreeable—they *must come*, and I will meet them that I may know them upon the stage just for the first time.

L. performed with many other hypnotists, professional and amateur. Among the latter were the author of a book on hypnotism which has been somewhat favourably noticed in the British press, and a well-known 'faith-healing' divine. It is all the same story, *mutato nomine.*

Whether L. actually gulled the various 'professors,' 'Drs.,' &c., to whose influence he submitted, as completely as he states may be doubted, and in any case the matter is of no interest to anyone but those who may have paid their shillings and half-crowns on the understanding that they were to see a thaumaturgic display of a genuine kind. The case is different, however, as regards members of the medical profession whom he professes to have deceived. That he actually has succeeded in imposing on certain doctors is beyond question, but the evidence before me in no way bears out the statement made in 'Truth,' that L. 'had again and again solemnly been experimented on by eminent English doctors, and that he had simply made fools of them all.' On the other hand it is clear that he succeeded in humbugging the editor of 'Truth' himself. After speaking of a 'learned caucus' at St. Mary's Hospital, where 'some medico performed the amazing feat of raising a blister upon him [L.] by mere "suggestion" while he [the subject] was under hypnotic control in the next room,' Mr. Labouchere goes on to say: 'If that worthy medico could have heard the youth describe to me how he raised the blister, I think he would have taken down his brass plate forthwith, and have retired into private life for very shame. This "promising subject" further bore on his body the marks of a serious surgical operation, which, by his own account, he had undergone in France for an enormous fee at the hands of two doctors. Both of these votaries of science seem to have been so anxious to test the possibility of performing the operation on a hypnotised patient that they quite omitted the preliminary formality of ascertaining whether the patient was not quite as wide awake as themselves.' While admitting that he has only the patient's word for this edifying story, the editor of 'Truth' makes it clear that he fully believes, or at least sees nothing improbable in it, a suggestive circumstance which seems to show that after all there may be something in hypnotism.

There can be no doubt, however, that L. found some of his most confiding dupes among members of the medical profession. Speaking of one of these, a demonstrator of physiology at a London medical school, L. says:

This gentleman I first met at the Royal Aquarium after leaving the stage. He made an appointment with me at his house and tried to mesmerise me. The first time I did not let him succeed entirely, next time the same, but the third time he succeeded to get me under his entire control. He mesmerized me always with his *eye-glasses* on, and that made me sometimes laugh in his face. He asked me the reason and I replied he looked at me so stern, that made me laugh. He made any number of difficult experiments on me, viz. making me write my name at different ages like 7 years, 9, 12, 15, and 19 years of age. He used to put me to sleep and make an impression on my mind that as soon as he rapped on the table I have to wake. There were then always three gentlemen present, but I always succeeded. He also gave me ink to drink, and tested my pulse on a pulse-tester machine ; while there he did the blister trick. Of course Mr. —— was a very firm believer in mesmerism. I have heard nothing of him lately. At his place I met Dr. —— of —— Hospital, where I gave a show. —— did all sorts of tricks with me. He also experimented heavily with an electric battery. He made me fetch certain books from the book-case ; also when he touched a flower to fall asleep. He made me a teetotalar [*sic*], and I promised to remain one. He also put an impression on me never to be mesmerised again by anyone. Of course, all these things never come true.

Poor Mr. —— would seem to have been fooled to the top of his bent; and from the correspondence which his tricky subject placed in my hands he would seem to have paid, one way or the other, a good deal of money for the imposition practised upon him. He may, I think, be taken as a type of the scientific man who is led astray when he touches hypnotism and cognate subjects, not so much by the want of knowledge or power of observation, as by what I should call want of insight into character to control the merely scientific judgment.

Being curious to study the *technique* of so exceptionally gifted an artist as L., I accepted his offer. to use his own elegant language, 'to give a show' at my house. I invited several medical acquaintances interested in hypnotism, including Dr. J. Milne Bramwell, Dr. Hack Tuke, Dr. Outterson Wood, Surgeon-Colonel J. B. Hamilton, Mr. Wingfield, and others, to be present on the occasion. L. brought two other subjects with him : one of these was introduced by him as his cousin, but there was so strong a family likeness between all the three, that they might easily have passed for brothers. There are few people who, as Sydney Smith said of Francis Horner, 'have the Ten Commandments written on their faces.' It is, therefore, not the fault of these ingenuous youths that their physiognomy is not exactly, to put it delicately, such

as would generally be accepted as a guarantee of good
faith.   They went through all their ordinary ' platform '
business, simulating the hypnotic sleep, performing
various antics ' under control,' and in particular ' going
through catalepsy,' to use my friend's own phrase.   Not
the least interesting part of the ' show ' was the preliminary hypnotisation of L. by the demonstrator of
physiology already referred to, whose eyes had not yet
been opened to the fact that he had been imposed upon.
When he commanded L. to ' sleep ' the latter obediently
did so, with all the usual appearances of profound
hypnotisation, muscular relaxation, facial congestion,
upturned eyeballs, not moving when touched, apparent
insensibility, stertor, insensibility to sound, light, and
external stimuli.   The performance was splendid and
complete, and Mr. —— enjoyed a moment's triumph.
But L. instantly woke up again with a leer as soon as
the operator announced that he was ' under influence.'
Mr. —— made several further attempts to hypnotise
his former subject, each time with the same result.
The situation was comic, yet had in it an element of
pathos ; the operator was so earnest a believer that the
shock of his awakening was almost painful to witness.

L.'s performance was not destitute of merit, but to
the critical judgment it left a good deal to be desired.
He overdid his part, the congestion of his face being
exaggerated to a degree almost suggestive of impending
apoplexy, while his snoring somewhat overstepped the
modesty of nature.   These points were dwelt on by

more than one of the gentlemen present, but I am not altogether free from a suspicion that in some of the cases at least the observation was of an *ex post facto* nature. On the whole, it was a very clever, but somewhat overdone, imitation of the ordinary hypnotic sleep.

One of L.'s companions seemed to me to simulate the hypnotic sleep better than he did, but L. at once dispelled any illusion there might have been by unexpectedly gripping him behind the knee. Some exhibitions of 'post-hypnotic suggestion' given by the two were well calculated to tickle the groundlings in a music hall, but could hardly have deceived any serious observer. The 'catalepsy business' had more artistic merit. So rigid did L. make his muscles that he could be lifted in one piece like an Egyptian mummy. He lay with his head on the back of one chair, and his heels on another, and allowed a fairly heavy man to sit on his stomach ; it seemed to me, however, that he was here within a 'straw' or two of the limit of his endurance. The 'blister trick' spoken of by 'Truth' as having deceived some medical men was done by rapidly biting and sucking the skin of the wrist. L. did manage with some difficulty to raise a slight swelling, but the marks of the teeth were plainly visible.

As to the wonderful operation on his throat, L. made a great mystery of it, and required a good deal of pressing before he could be induced to allow the scar to be seen. The reason of this unexpected modesty was apparent as soon as the part was shown, for the wound had obviously been self-inflicted. How anyone could have imagined that such a wound had been made by a surgeon's hand, it is difficult to understand. When challenged on the subject, L. took refuge in the supposed *sub sigillo* nature of the transaction, a sudden awakening of conscientious scruples which was in amusing contrast with the extreme freedom of his voluntary confidences on all other matters relating to his professional experiences. Though the appearance of the scar itself was conclusive, the true nature of the ' operation ' was abundantly proved by the evidence of the records of the Royal Free Hospital, Gray's Inn Road, which, by a kind of poetical justice, the much-beguiled Mr. —— was the means of bringing to light.

One point in L.'s exhibition which was undoubtedly genuine was his remarkable and stoical endurance of pain. He stood before us smiling and open-eyed while he ran long needles into the fleshy parts of his arms and legs without flinching, and he allowed one of the gentlemen present to pinch his skin in different parts with strong crenated pincers in a manner which bruised it, and which to most people would have caused intense pain. L. allowed no sign of suffering or discomfort to appear ; he did not set his teeth or wince ; his pulse was not quickened, and the pupil of his eye did not dilate as physiologists tell us it does when pain passes a certain limit. It may be said that this merely shows that in L. the limit of endurance was beyond the normal standard, or, in other words, that his sensitiveness was less than that of the average man. At any rate, his performance in this respect was so remarkable that some of the gentlemen present were fain to explain it by a supposed 'post-hypnotic suggestion,' the theory apparently being that L. and his comrades hypnotised one another, and thus made themselves insensible to pain. Such a power would have been invaluable to the Jews whose grinders were extracted by our Plantagenet kings, and to the heretics who fell into the clutches of the Inquisition. So far-fetched an explanation is, however, unnecessary. As surgeons have reason to know, persons vary widely in their sensitiveness to pain. I have seen a man chat quietly with the bystanders while his carotid artery was being tied without the use of chloroform. During the Russo-Turkish war, wounded Turks often astonished English doctors by undergoing the most formidable amputations with no other anæsthetic than a cigarette. Hysterical women will inflict very severe pain on themselves—merely for wantonness or in order to excite sympathy. The fakirs who allow themselves to be hung up by hooks beneath their shoulder-blades seem to think little of it, and, as a matter of fact, I believe are not much inconvenienced by the process.

The impression left on my mind by L.'s performance was mainly a feeling of wonder that so vulgar and transparent a piece of trickery should ever have imposed on anyone. Yet, though having no scientific interest in itself, the 'show' has a *foolometric* value of a very distinct kind. That any medical man should have thought ' phenomena ' such as those obligingly displayed by these subjects worthy of serious study is, as Carlyle would have said, ' significant of much.' What weight can be attached to the judgment of persons so devoid of the critical faculty when dealing with these matters ? If they allow themselves to be gulled by so sorry an impostor as L., are they not likely to be as wax in the hands of subjects of a higher order, in whom a natural genius for deception has been developed, and I may say educated, by the unconscious tuition of scientific enthusiasts ? I am willing to believe that some subjects may, like Hamlet, be ' indifferent honest,' at least at first ; but it must be as difficult for a person who is habitually made the subject of such experiments to remain truthful as for a publican to be a total abstainer. The wish to please the investigator leads in the first instance to a little over-colouring ; then come a harmless experiment or two on the scientific pundit's credulity, and so on, the appetite for deception growing by that it feeds on, to systematic imposture. Men are easily induced to see what they are anxious to see, and even the dry light of science does not always keep its votaries out of this pitfall. ' Suggestion ' often acts more powerfully on the operator than on the subject.

It is not too much to say that the majority of observations of hypnotic phenomena which we are invited to accept on the authority of men of acknowledged scientific competence and indisputable personal integrity are vitiated by the fundamental assumption that the subjects are trustworthy—that is, neither deceiving nor self-deceived. This source of fallacy is one to which the scientific experimenter is perhaps peculiarly exposed. He is rather apt to look upon his subjects as the pathologists look upon their rabbits and guinea-pigs, simply as the abstract quantities, x, y, or z, in a scientific theorem, without taking into acount the possible disturbing influence of the 'personal equation.' In investigating the phenomena of hypnotism, scientific phenomena must always be controlled and directed by the practical insight of the man of the world, and a cardinal principle in all such inquiries must be to look upon all experiments on trained mediums or hysterical subjects as utterly worthless. How even the best trained scientific judgment may be misled by disregard of this fundamental truth was only too well illustrated by the example of Charcot, who finally abandoned his researches in this department of neurology in disgust.

The rules of scientific criticism which should guide us in estimating the value of such experiments cannot be better formulated than they have been by Professor Moriz Benedikt of Vienna, in the following sentences : ' 1. Hypnotic phenomena in general cannot be accepted as scientifically established facts *without objective proof*. Performances at the command, or at the supposed wish, of the experimenter take place under the pressure of his authority, even in the case of persons who are not deliberate deceivers, relatively few persons being capable of independent volition and independent thought. 2. Only experiments on unprepared individuals who have not been initiated into the mysteries of hypnotism have any value; experiments on 'mediums' are worthless. 3. As a rule, only very few individuals and very few conditions are suitable for hypnotic treatment.' [1]

Professor Benedikt adds—and the vast majority of the medical profession will agree with him—that the repetition of such experiments on neurotic subjects cannot be too strongly condemned. Systematic hypnotisation is not only useless, but actively harmful, as it has ' a demoralising influence on the intellect, the will, and the psychical independence of the subject.'

While, however, admitting, as I have already said, that hypnotism is a reality, I repeat that the great bulk of the ' phenomena ' described by observers reputed to be ' scientific ' is founded on imposture. What is true in hypnotism is not new—for it is only old-fashioned mesmerism masquerading under a newly coined Greek name—nor is it of any practical use to mankind. The ' cures ' attributed to its agency are exactly similar to those wrought by ' faith-healing,' when they are not altogether imaginary.

---

[1] ' Hypnotismus und Suggestion : eine klinisch-psychologische Studio.' Leipzig und Wien, 1894.

APPENDIX

—◆>◄—

In view of the re-assertion by M. Encausse in the 'Revue
de Psychiatrie' of the absolutely incorrect statement that
the persons on whom I experimented were any other
than the actual subjects introduced to me by Dr. Luys
himself at the Charité, and the pretension that they were
persons whom Dr. Luys had discarded, I think it well to
reprint the letters from Dr. Luys and myself which were
published in the 'Times,' and in which Dr. Luys, after
having brought forward that unfounded statement, was
unable to support it. Two of the subjects on whom I
experimented were actual patients in the wards ; they
were all five the subjects, and the only subjects, on whom
Dr. Luys gave his demonstrations to myself and to a
number of journalists and medical men in December and
January, and three of them were subjects on whom he had
continuously lectured for many years, and whose various
performances will be found figured and described at
great length in his papers and Clinical Lectures to which
I have referred in the text. Clarice and Jeanne especially
are reproduced in a great number of photographs. Jeanne,
whose letter I print on p. 143, is perhaps the most har-
dened and elaborate impostor of the series, and she is the
central figure in the photographs on pp. 97 and 99, and
which Dr. Luys gave me with his own hands, having brought

them, as he said, for me, to illustrate the striking effects of attraction and repulsion by the two ends of the magnetic bars ; a phenomenon which I proved, and invited him to prove, by very simple means, to be pure fraud. Having declined to apply any of the very simple tests suggested to him by me in the wards, by which he could easily have ascertained for himself the thorough imposture of his subjects, it ill becomes Dr. Luys to complain that I was incompetent, or that in applying simple and accurate scientific tests I was doing anything more than he ought to have done long since out of respect to his own assumed position of a man of science, and to the honour of the science of medicine and the reputation of the great hospital which the continuance of these fictitious performances seriously discredits.

THE NEW MESMERISM

TO THE EDITOR OF THE 'TIMES'

Sir,—Having been invited by the committee of the Institut de France to attend the Pasteur Jubilee, I found myself in Paris at the moment when the first communication of your correspondent on 'The New Mesmerism' was published. In view of the importance attaching to statements published so prominently and with so much detail in the columns of the 'Times,' I took the opportunity of communicating through a medical friend with Dr. Luys, and was invited by him to witness the demonstrations which your correspondent so picturesquely describes, and which carried such firm conviction to his mind. The whole phenomena which he witnessed were actually reproduced before me, and many more, still more startling and dramatic, of which he makes no mention. Being deeply interested in performances which were, *primâ facie*, so astounding, and which, if verified, would carry us back to some of the old practices and conclusions of the mystics and sorcerers of the middle ages, I thought it worth while to spend a fortnight in the closest investigation of the facts, and in attempting to arrive at correct conclusions as to their causation.

With this object I made repeated visits to La Charité Hospital, and I visited the École Polytechnique by the invitation of Colonel Rochas d'Aiglun, the head of the school, who reproduced before me there, as he had already done in the presence of Dr. Luys at La Charité Hospital, the performances described as 'externalisation of the sensations' and 'transference of sensibility to inanimate objects.' I was able to carry out at La Charité itself some very simple test experiments, which, at the outset, convinced me that Dr. Luys was the victim, to some extent, of trickery and imposture, and that he did not take even the elementary precautions necessary to protect himself from fraud on the part of his subjects, and from self-deception. I suggested to him at once one or two simple tests of the good faith of his patients, such as the use of an electro-magnet, in which the magnetic current could easily be extinguished without the patient's knowledge ; and again, in his experiments on the influence or alleged influence of medicinal substances in sealed tubes placed in contact with the skin, I suggested that substances other than those which the patient had reason to believe were in use should actually be applied. Both of these precautions, however, he declined to take at the time, alleging either that he had done so in the past or would do so in the future. He could only show me, he said, his experiments in his own way, and if I were not convinced, he could only regret it. On each of the occasions of my visits I was accompanied by independent and competent witnesses, who observed with me that in two instances in which I employed very simple magnetic tests of control, the patients were utterly at fault, giving false answers, and seeing blue flames and red flames issue from a small pocket similimagnet, which was no magnet at all, and making other blunders which equally gave reason to suspect imposture.

Subsequently to this I secured the attendance at my apartments of five of the persons on whom Dr. Luys had been and is still accustomed to give his demonstrations in the wards, and who have been the chief subjects of his 'Leçons Cliniques,' of which I have before me the printed volumes, containing reports of the marvellous phenomena produced, with photographic representations of many of them. I had in all nearly twelve sittings with these five subjects, among them being the persons shown to your correspondent and going through the performances which he describes. At all these sittings there were present medical and scientific witnesses and independent observers of undoubted competency. Among those who were present at one or other of the sittings were Dr. Louis Olivier, Docteur-ès-Sciences, Directeur de la 'Revue Générale des Sciences'; Dr. Lutaud, editor of the 'Journal de Médecine de Paris'; Dr. Sajous, editor of the American 'Annual of Medicine'; M. Cremière, of St. Petersburg; Mr. B. F. C. Costelloe, of London, and others whose names I need not at present mention. They have signed the notes of the various test experiments. These notes are too numerous and too detailed to permit me to venture to burden your columns with them ; I shall shortly publish them in detail. I need only say here that the whole of the phenomena were produced with sham magnets, with substituted figures, with misnamed medicinal substances, and with distilled water, and with sham 'suggestion,' opposite suggestion, or none at all. Everyone was able to convince himself that all the results so shown were, without exception, simulated, fictitious, and fraudulent. That some of the patients were hypnotic and hysterical in a high degree does not alter the fact that from beginning to end they all showed themselves to be tricksters of the most barefaced kind ; some of them very clever actors, possessing dramatic powers which might have been turned to better purposes, most of them utterly venal, and some of them confessing that they played upon the credulity of Dr. Luys for their own purposes.

I do not of course ask your readers to accept this statement as final evidence, but the protocols of the sittings, signed by the witnesses present at each of them, and the detail of the methods employed will, I think, convince even the most credulous apostles of the new mesmerism that we have here to deal only with another chapter of human folly, misled by fraud ; a reproduction of the old frauds of Mesmer, of the self-deceptions of Reichenbach, and the malpractices of sham magicians of the middle ages who have still their ingenious imitators. These impostures and this self-deception now mask themselves under a new nomenclature, and avail themselves of recent developments of psychological investigation in order to assume more plausible shapes and a *pseudo*-scientific character. But when the authentic details of their separate and combined simulations are read, it will only remain to regret that so much prominence has been given to so sad a page in human wickedness and folly, and that men of distinguished position and good faith have allowed themselves, by carelessness and persistent credulity, to be made use of as propagators and apostles of wild follies and vulgar deceptions. There is a still more painful social and moral side to this matter to

which I can here only distantly allude, but which confirms
me in the belief that the question is at least as much one of
police as of science, and from that point of view deserves
the attention of the lay authorities of the Paris hospitals
and of the correctional tribunals.

I am, Sir, your obedient servant,

ERNEST HART.

'British Medical Journal,' 429 Strand, W.C., January 9, 1893.

DR. LUYS'S REPLY TO MR. HART

TO THE EDITOR OF THE 'TIMES'

Sir,—Mr. Hart, in a former article which appeared a
few weeks ago, attacked me most violently on the subject
of some hypnotical experiments which I made in his presence
at the Hôpital de la Charité.

As Mr. Hart had shown me he was perfectly incompetent as judge of the matter, that he was even ignorant
of the primary elements of the problem, such as the different states undergone by hypnotised patients, I concluded
it was useless to waste my time by discussion with a mere
amateur, and thus did not reply to assertions which I
considered of no value whatever.

He has returned to the subject in a fresh article, full
of malevolent insinuations and intended inaccuracy ; further, he incriminates my honour as a man of science,
coupling my name with epithets which I am surprised to
find traced by his pen.   I consider myself, therefore,
obliged to break silence, so that the public may not remain
under the influence of this extra-scientific attack.

Mr. Hart has simply mixed up, in his wrath, my
personal experiments and those undertaken by my

fellow-worker and friend, Colonel de Rochas, and that because they took place at the hospital in my consulting room.

In his presence I merely gave a few simple experiments and demonstrations—showing him, for instance, that when persons are hypnotised their usual faculties are raised to an extra-physiological pitch, and that the patients see things that we cannot in our normal state distinguish ; thus they behold the waves which are developed from a polarised bar and from a magnetic needle with their different colouring. In order to demonstrate the physical fact, I told him that the examination of the back of the eye, before the hypnotic state, and also during that state, by the aid of the ophthalmoscope, showed to any observer that the retina, which is pale before the operation, became instantaneously red, there being a violent determination of blood to it during the somnambulistic state, and that at the same time the possibilities of accommodation of the eye are destroyed. This is an indisputable criterion which explains the increase of the visual power, and I am not aware that this purely objective phenomenon could be caused in a fraudulent manner.

I also went through (in presence of Mr. Hart) some experiments relative to the psychical action, either attractive or repulsive, of the different poles of a magnetic bar on hypnotised patients. I also showed him that glass tubes, containing either brandy or tincture of valerian, applied to the same patients, could determine on them effects peculiar to those substances.

Such were the personal experiments, accomplished in presence of Mr. Hart, and which he seemed to accept with approval. And I ask all people of good faith—Is there in this anything contrary to scientific morality, and which represents, as Mr. Hart emphatically states, a lamentable page of human folly, calling for the intervention of the police magistrate? *Risum teneatis amici?*

Pursuing the campaign, Mr. Hart has deemed it necessary to make a few personal experiments on his own account (I am persuaded he knew nothing of the scientific direction of these experiments) and in a private residence, so as to be able to make these fantastic investigations quite at his ease, and under the pretext of controlling what he had seen at La Charité. He was unlucky enough to apply to patients whom I have long ceased to have recourse to, being unable to depend on their veracity. He questioned them privately, he believed solemnly in their declarations, without having a notion that these patients are so passive that the questioner can make them say anything he chooses, the most unlikely things—even, for instance, that Mr. Hart's labours in hypnotism are of the very first order. His inexperience here made him fall into the very grossest snare.

All the other experiments belonging to the exteriorisation of sensitiveness, so vehemently criticised by Mr. Hart, by means of extra-scientific processes, do not belong to me. They are real and, I confess, extraordinary discoveries made by my fellow-labourer and friend, Colonel de Rochas, whose patient researches have been most justly appreciated by most competent men.

Briefly, all these simple things are really not worth so much rhetoric.

I am, Sir, your most obedient servant,

Dr. J. Luys,

Member of the Académie de Médecine (French College of Surgeons), Doctor of the Hospital of La Charité.

Paris, 20 rue de Grenelle, January 24, 1893.

DR. LUYS AND HIS PATIENTS

TO THE EDITOR OF THE 'TIMES'

Sir,—M. Luys rushes on his own sword. I was careful
to avoid saying anything which should impugn his scientific
honour. He now raises that perilous issue, and stands self-
impeached in your columns by his own words and by no
will of mine. When did Dr. Luys become convinced of
'the want of veracity' of the patients whom I have detected
and denounced as impostors? He says it is long since;
but the persons on whom I operated, and whose futile
frauds I exposed, were the very persons on whom he showed,
on several occasions between December 28 and January 6,
to me and others what he speaks of as the 'simple phenomena' of magnetic attraction and repulsion; of visual
perception of coloured flames from the magnet, from photographs and prints, and from the human face; the storage
of thought in a head circlet; the cat performance, the
tipsy scene, the transference of drunkenness by contact, and
those on whom Colonel de Rochas showed at the Charité
what Dr. Luys describes as real 'facts,' the transference of
sensibility to the air, to a glass of water, and to a wax doll.
The whole performance has turned out to be a pure
comedy. But if Dr. Luys has long been conscious of the
unveracity of the subjects who play these antics, I am at a
loss to explain the fact that up to January 5 he was presenting them to myself, to his students, and to journalists and
visitors as sincere subjects. Their names are Marguerite,
Jeanne, Clarice, and Mervel. It is Dr. Luys himself who
now comes forward to proclaim that his performances were
on 'untrustworthy subjects.' It is a very serious position
which he thus creates for himself.

As to the completeness and convincing nature of my control demonstrations, anyone may form a judgment who is sufficiently interested by reading the details in the current number of the 'Nineteenth Century,' or in the series of illustrated reports in course of publication in the 'British Medical Journal.'

From the evidence of the eye-witnesses of my experiments I select the letters of two eminent scientists—Dr. de Cyon, one of the most eminent of physiologists, and Dr. L. Olivier, D.Sc., Directeur of the 'Revue Générale des Sciences.'

Dr. de Cyon writes, under date of January 28, 1893 :—

'I can testify that the experiments at which I was present took place exactly as you have described them in your letter to the "Times." The methods which you employed to demonstrate the trickery on the part of the subjects— notably the changing of the dolls and the substitution of the glass of water and of the magnet—are of such simplicity that one finds a difficulty in believing that the physicians who have made themselves the apostles of this new superstition are acting in good faith. I have myself made numerous experiments on Dr. Luys's subjects and on those of many other physicians, and I have always succeeded with the greatest facility in unmasking their frauds, which really can only deceive those who wish to be deceived. Either dupes or accomplices—there is no other alternative for the adepts of the doctrines which are now tending to discredit medicine and to throw it back many centuries. I am entirely in agreement with you on what you have said as to the morality of the subjects who lend themselves to these grotesque experiments. All this concerns much more the *police des mœurs* rather than clinical medicine.'

Dr. Louis Olivier writes, under date January 19, 1893 :—

'I am quite ready to relate what I saw at the sittings which took place in your room in the Hôtel Continental. There was no agreement between the phenomena manifested by the hypnotised subjects and the production of the current of magnetisation, &c. You repeated the experiments of Dr. Luys and those of M. de Rochas, avoiding all suggestion, either involuntary or unconscious, which might vitiate the results. You took care to hide from the subjects the nature of the drugs tested, to which M. Luys attributes an action at a distance, the moment of the closure or opening of the current of your electro-magnet. Under these conditions there was no longer any relation between the nature of the medicinal agent and the symptoms manifested ; when the circuit was opened without their knowledge the subjects said they experienced the varied sensations which they ordinarily attribute to the passage of the current. They were unable to distinguish the open from the closed state of the current. You repeated M. de Rochas's experiment of *envoûtement*, employing without the knowledge of the hypnotised woman two dolls, one of which remained carefully separated from the sleeping woman. The latter uttered shrieks when I pulled the hair of the doll which she had not touched, &c. These facts appear to me decisive for the settlement of a question which I ought to say has been decided by the vast majority of the French scientific public in a sense absolutely opposed to the results proclaimed by MM. Luys and de Rochas. It is well that it should be known in England that the opinion of these two experimenters finds no support in the French scientific world.'

I invited Dr. Luys and Colonel de Rochas to be present

at a final repetition of my experiments.   Colonel de Rochas
came ; Dr. Luys excused himself from being present.

I am, Sir, yours faithfully,

ERNEST HART.

'British Medical Journal,' 429 Strand, February 1, 1893.

THE ETERNAL GULLIBLE

THERE can be no more striking illustration of the readiness
with which persons of highly cultivated mind may be
misled by vulgar impostors than the recent performances
of Eusapia Paladino at Cambridge.   In connection with
this subject the following article appeared in the 'British
Medical Journal' of November 9, 1895 :—

EXIT EUSAPIA !

The collapse of Eusapia Paladino, one of the chief
priestesses of the latter-day occultism, is highly satisfactory
to all lovers of truth as the exposure of a particularly
impudent system of imposture.   The event has a much
greater importance, however, as an additional exposure of
the facility with which cultivated minds of a certain type
can be cozened by clever trickery.   It takes little to delude
them, because their 'suggestibility' (if the word may be
allowed) makes themselves active helpers in the process.
The maxim *Populus vult decipi* applies to philosophers not
less than to the vulgar ; they believe because they wish to
believe.   Nothing can be more amusing to a cynic than to
see persons, often of a high order of intelligence, accept the
foolish wonders of spirit-rapping and table-turning with a
simple faith which they scornfully refuse to more sacred

mysteries. For years, men skilled in all the learning of schools and trained to some extent in scientific observation have been sitting at the feet of this illiterate woman, reverently waiting for the stirring of the muddy waters of deception, which they eagerly drink in as manifestations of a 'new psychic force.' It would be comic if it were not deplorable to picture this sorry Egeria surrounded by men like Professor Sidgwick, Professor Lodge, Mr. F. H. Myers, Dr. Schiaparelli, and Professor Richet, solemnly receiving her pinches and kicks, her finger skiddings, her sleight of hand with various articles of furniture as phenomena calling for serious study, if not as direct revelations of the Unseen. It is saddest of all to think of Lombroso, who must know more than most men of human imposture, in this circle of devotees.

> Who could not laugh if such a man there be ?
> Who but must weep if Atticus were he?

The fact is, however, as was pointed out by Mr. Ernest Hart in his article on The Eternal Gullible in the 'Century,' men of science are not as such particularly well qualified to judge of matters in which the disturbing influence of the 'personal equation' has to be taken into account. They are apt to be misled by starting from the assumption that all persons may be taken, for the purposes of experiment, as equally trustworthy. In studying the phenomena of occultism of any kind, it is essential to bear in mind that there is a twofold source of fallacy—in the facts and in the interpretation thereof. Everything that appears to be inexplicable is not necessarily supernatural. What is wanted before everything else is the detective skill of the expert. Had Mr. Maskelyne not been present at the recent sitting at Cambridge, Eusapia's shrine would probably not have been deserted even now. Indeed, there is Professor Lodge, ' of the unfaithful, faithful only he,' whose robust faith in the earlier manifestations is still undisturbed. And yet the whole thing is such a transparent fraud! Else why all these jealous precautions, extending to details of dress? Why all this careful darkening of the stage before the performance unless it be because the children of darkness hate the light? Then, what can be more childish, more utterly futile, than the manifestations themselves? The silly games at 'touch,' and the purposeless evolutions of chairs and tables might amuse a child of five at a pantomime, but what is to be said of learned professors, and earnest and otherwise intelligent men and women, seeking spiritual edification in such foolery? Is any human being likely to be the better or the wiser for the rappings of 'John' or the scribblings of 'Julia'? With so many serious problems awaiting solution it is not only deplorable but in the highest degree discreditable that minds made for better things should waste their powers in dabbling with what is simply despicable and degrading imposture.

To this article Professor Sidgwick replied in the 'British Medical Journal,' November 16, 1895, as follows :—

Sir,—My attention has been drawn to an article in the 'British Medical Journal,' of November 9, in which reference is made to experiments with Eusapia Paladino in which I have taken part. In the course of the article it is implied that I and the other investigators mentioned 'accepted the foolish wonders of spirit-rapping and table-turning with simple faith,' and as 'direct revelations from the Unseen,' and sought 'spiritual edification' from them. It is further affirmed that 'had Mr. Maskelyne not been present at the recent sittings at Cambridge, Eusapia's shrine would probably not have been deserted even now.'

I must ask leave to state that these statements and implications are one and all entirely without foundation so far as I am concerned. I have never accepted the wonders of spirit-rapping and table-turning ; and if I had, I should never have sought spiritual edification from them. The trickery, which the experiments at Cambridge proved to have been used by Eusapia, had been long ago suggested by Professor Richet himself, and more recently had been precisely and fully described by Mr. Richard Hodgson, the secretary of the American branch of the Society for Psychical Research, in a paper criticising the conclusions of the Italian *savants* and of Professor Lodge. It was to test the issue thus raised between two members of our group of investigators—Professor Lodge and Mr. Hodgson—that the experiments at Cambridge were arranged. Mr. Hodgson himself took part in them, and they ended in entirely confirming the opinion that he had previously expressed. And though I set a high value on Mr. Maskelyne's acumen and skill, his intervention in this case did not in fact affect the progress of the investigation.

I may add that the general drift of your article shows a complete ignorance of the work in which the group of investigators to which I belong have been engaged since the foundation of the Society for Psychical Research thirteen years ago. Throughout this period we have continually combated and exposed the frauds of professional mediums, and have never yet published in our 'Proceedings,' any report in favour of the performances of any of them.

I am, &c.,

HENRY SIDGWICK.

Cambridge, November 12, 1895.

To this letter the following editorial note was appended :—

We gladly accept Professor Sidgwick's assurance that he does not accept the wonders of spirit-rapping, and that

he has not sought spiritual edification from them. This
being so, however, we would respectfully ask, *Que diable est-
il allé faire dans cette galère?* If the Society for Psychical
Research do not seek for signs and wonders, what go they
out for to see? We can understand the position of those
weaker brethren, who expect to find evidence of a future
life in mysterious taps and pinches, but how men like our
distinguished correspondent and his colleagues can think
such rubbish worth investigating as 'phenomena' or 'manifestations of psychic force' passes our comprehension. As
regards Mr. Maskelyne's share in the exposure of Eusapia,
there appears to be a difference of opinion between that
gentleman and Professor Sidgwick, and we must leave them
to settle the matter between them. It is a fact that Mr.
Maskelyne was, apparently at the suggestion of Mr. Andrew
Lang, called in to assist in unveiling the prophetess, and
we may add that we entirely agree with Mr. Lang in relying
more on the conjurer than on the psychical researchers.
As regards the work of the Society for Psychical Research,
our complaint against it is not that it publishes reports in
favour of the performances of professional mediums, but
that it wastes time which might be given to the solution of
problems urgently concerning the welfare of mankind in
the investigation of phenomena which have their origin in
delusion, when they are not the result of jugglery and
imposture, and which in any case are unworthy of the
notice of serious men.

———

THE HYPNOTISM OF 'TRILBY'

[*From the* BRITISH MEDICAL JOURNAL, *November* 20, 1895]

MR. ERNEST HART writes : 'Trilby' as a drama by no means
corresponds in the development of its hypnotic motive and
action with the originally artistic and yet scientifically

well-drawn conception of Mr. Du Maurier in his novel. It is, perhaps, dramatically more effective, but it is the hypnotism of the platform and the stage play, and not that of Nature and pathology. In the 'Trilby' of Mr. Du Maurier, the influence of direct, open, and positive suggestion, which is the real working power of all 'hypnotic' conditions, is the mainspring of the action. The all-sufficient subjective change wrought by this agency is admirably used and developed with subtlety and fine literary effect. In the stage version a new hypnotism appears. Svengali— a magnificent study by Mr. Beerbohm Tree of the weird, unclean, spider-like mesmerist of the school of the popular imagination—a twentieth century Mephistopheles—possesses all the mystic powers of the mystery worker of romance, with a suggestion of decadent demonism. As an impersonation it is one of the highest efforts of histrionic skill seen in modern times. Svengali has a 'force' which he passes into Trilby ; he hypnotises her from behind unseen ; he draws her to him from another room by 'force of will' ; he is exhausted by the transference to her of 'his life.' All this is very effective from the stage point of view, but it clothes a vulgar error with the glamour of genius, and it possibly may renew for a time the vogue of the follies and frauds of the sham 'hypnotism, mesmerism, and new magic,' which I had hoped almost to have driven from the notice of reasonable men. Meantime all London will be drawn to see a most remarkable presentment of the platform 'mesmerist' outwardly at his best, or at his worst. Miss Baird's beautiful personality and well-conceived presentation of the hypnotised pupil and victim of Svengali is most attractive and remarkable for some fine touches of intuition and observation.

[*From the* BRITISH MEDICAL JOURNAL, *November* 16, 1895]

The pivot on which Mr. Du Maurier's extremely able and popular book depends is a hypnotic phenomenon of which the publicity is adversely criticised in many well-informed quarters. Mr. Ernest Hart, however, the author of 'Hypnotism, Mesmerism, and the New Witchcraft,' of which no small part is devoted to exposing many of the shams and impostures exhibited and described under that title, is of opinion that while Mr. Du Maurier has with dramatic and artistic instincts somewhat stretched the working probabilities of hypnotic condition beyond the ordinary limits, and has artistically concealed the difficulties and mechanism by which his striking effects are produced, he has, nevertheless, not outstepped the bounds of possibility. Of course, to the uninformed critic and observer, the mere fact of the apparent endowment of Trilby, under the influence of suggestion, with powers and capacities which she does not possess otherwise or at other times than when placed under this influence, appears either miraculous or false, or suggestive of some new force, some transference of nerve power, or some so-called magnetic influence, to use the ordinary jargon. Those who have followed Charcot, or who agree with Mr. Hart in his analysis of the phenomena known as suggestion or hypnotism, hold that no such agencies exist, and the phenomena such as those which the hypnotic state presents are due to the transformation effected in a perfectly natural and physiological manner in the subject under the influence of external or auto-mental suggestion. It is by no means uncommon—and of this many instances have been widely observed, and are recorded in Mr. Hart's book—to find persons who, under the influence of suggestion, and when in the deep hypnotic state, are capable of feats of strength and of agility, of intense dramatic expression and matchless emotional effects, as may be seen in the photographs which have appeared in our columns when these articles were running through them, or in their collected form in the book itself. Superficially and at first sight it might appear that some new quality has been added, and some mental endowment, as it were, freshly injected into the subject; on more careful study, this is found not to be so. The ordinary individual is impeded in such dangerous efforts as leaping on narrow ledges, climbing the walls of a room, or in adopting the rapidly changing and intensely emotional attitudes and expressions by the inhibitory influence of fear or shyness and interfering mental emotion, and of other jarring and inhibitory influences. In the hypnotic state and under the influence of suggestion inhibition ceases, the individual is unconscious of danger, and *pro tanto* insusceptible of fear. The shyness, the awkwardness, the want of muscular exactness and intensity of effort produced by these interfering agencies are removed, and the subject becomes a machine wholly under the control of the expressed will from without with which there is nothing to interfere. The elaborate lessons of Svengali in vocalisation and dramatic passion might quite conceivably transform Trilby, who possesses a magnificent vocal organ, into a dramatic singer of the highest order. Under the conditions, which Mr. Du Maurier carefully and accurately indicates, of perfect hypnotic subjection, of complete abstraction from interfering external or internal influences, Trilby, when she sings, is in a perfect hypnotic sleep; she is unconscious of her audience and unaware of her surroundings. She is, like all thorough hypnotics, reduced to the state of a marvellous machine, capable of receiving the most perfect training and in complete subjection to the will and the suggestion of the

P

operator. The state is one of exaltation of certain muscular
and mental functions, due to the removal of all inhibitory
influences. It is quite characteristic that while in this
condition she performs the marvellous feat ascribed to her
in the book, but she has no recollection of anything she has
done while in this condition. When, however, the presence and the suggestive influence of her teacher are
removed, she relapses into complete and bewildered incom-
petency, for no new faculty has been added, no new mental
power has been given ; the influence is only that of training in the hypnotic state and under the suggestion, and
when these motor conditions are removed, she is no better,
but rather worse, in her last state than in her first.   Mr.
Du Maurier may be congratulated on having produced, for
the first time, a literary masterpiece in which the conditions
of hypnotism are used with the power of genius, and in
which their limitations and nature are correctly indicated
if not fully analysed or described.

AUTOMATIC WRITING

On the subject of the mechanism of automatic writing,
I may be allowed to reprint the following article which
appeared in the 'British Medical Journal' of November 4,
1893 :—

The 'Pall Mall Gazette' published recently an able
article on this subject by 'Hypnos,' and we are inclined to
think the subject is advanced one step by this writer.   It
is to be feared that not even a Commission would satisfy
the believers in the spook origin of the automatic writing
that it can be more readily explained in simpler ways.
The writer of the article points out that the chief elements
are unconscious movements, gradual education, and faith.

The result produced bears internal evidence of being very like the ordinary thoughts of the instrument—that is, the automaton. To explain how the unconscious scrawling can become intelligible sentences, he calls in two laws of suggestion, which come to this, that the conditions most suited for the writing are a weak-minded receptivity, a dominant idea, and the power of the dominating idea on the brain (? mind) through faith, training, and education. We agree with this as a whole, and we think the interpretation must be sought through sleep and hypnotic conditions. We all agree that an enormous mass of impressions are received by the senses ; many never become perceptions, yet they may have been recorded, and may under certain conditions be called into use. In delirium and in hypnotic states we see this. Disease may bring to a level of consciousness things which have never been reckoned as knowledge. In dreams we have clear revivals of impressions which seem altogether new things to us. Thus many a person has believed that he or some companion in his dreams has spoken a foreign language much better than he himself could speak it, and we have met with persons suffering from hallucinations of hearing, who have used it as an argument that the voices they heard were not their own imaginings, for, as they have said, they speak French better than they ever could. There are, then, stories of impressions, more or less organically connected with each other in the brain, which under certain diseased states may be brought to light, and it seems to be not only probable but certain that what is morbid in one person may be natural in another, so that the poet in his half-sleeping moments may compose and seem to commune with other beings. In some, probably, there is—by habit assisting a peculiar nature—a power to draw upon the unconscious store—the dream-stuff, to use a convenient phrase—of the brain, and once having granted this, it is not hard to suppose that the mechanical expression through the machine may be got very readily to work. The whole evolution of the writing, the slow beginning, the steady progress are all like the other mechanical developments; once start a train of thought the line is followed, without control, readily enough, as most men know who have allowed their thoughts to run away with them—the expression of these thoughts may be allowed to run more conspicuously through the machine, one movement readily leading to the next, and so on. This is true of thought, and is pretty certainly true of the established methods of expression. We are inclined, with the writer in the 'Pall Mall Gazette,' to think that this removal of higher control may be cultivated, but that there is danger in thus yielding up the reins. Many persons have begun earnestly to investigate spiritism only to be led away by their own fancies. This, of course, is not an argument against investigation, but it is an argument for exhausting every reasonable explanation before calling in spirits from the vasty deep or elsewhere.

PRINTED BY
SPOTTISWOODE AND CO., NEW-STREET SQUARE
LONDON

BY THE SAME AUTHOR.

---◆◆---

THE STATE AND ITS SERVANTS.
London: Smith, Elder, & Co.   One Shilling.

A WINTER TRIP TO 'THE FORTUNATE ISLANDS.'
Demy 8vo.   One Shilling.   London: Smith, Elder, & Co.

IS IT DESIRABLE TO TAKE ANY, AND WHAT
FURTHER MEASURES, TO PREVENT THE SPREAD
OF ZYMOTIC DISEASE THROUGH THE MILK SUPPLY
OF OUR TOWNS?   London: Smith, Elder, & Co.

THE INFLUENCE OF MILK IN SPREADING
ZYMOTIC DISEASE.   London: J. W. Kolckmann.

SPRAY FROM THE CARLSBAD SPRUDEL.
London: British Medical Association.

LECTURES ON JAPANESE ART WORKS.
London: Society of Arts.

ANCIENT AND MODERN ART POTTERY AND POR-
CELAIN OF JAPAN.   London: Society of Arts.

LOCAL GOVERNMENT, AS IT IS AND AS IT OUGHT
TO BE.   London: Smith, Elder, & Co.

THE TRUTH ABOUT VACCINATION.
London: Smith, Elder, & Co.

THE NURSERIES OF CHOLERA; its Diffusion and its
Extinction.   London: Smith, Elder, & Co.